OMENS

A COLLECTION

AARON DICK

CONTENTS

First Edition

Book Cover Art by Andy Dick
Book Cover Design by oliviaprodesign

ISBN 978-1-0670632-0-7 (Paperback)
ISBN 978-1-0670632-2-1 (eBook)
ISBN 978-1-0670632-1-4 (Kindle)

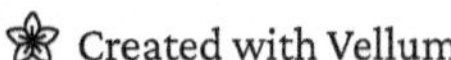 Created with Vellum

ALSO BY THIS AUTHOR:

Where The Fields Grow Light

When Hidden Eyes Grow Dim

Rotten

There Is A Stranger Here

This collection includes the entirety of two earlier digital-only releases.
Those were dedicated to
"everyone who has encouraged my writing; friends, family and colleagues"
and
"Steffocles; for her help and encouragement"
and so this collection is too.

ADOPTION

The calves were taken away today.
Rounded up and loaded onto the trailer,
into their wire cage.

Now their mothers moan,
call,
wail;
And I cannot sleep.

THIS QUIET ORPHEUS

ORIGINALLY PUBLISHED IN HEADLAND
ISSUE 20

It is my job to bring them back.

I CURL into the corner of our small couch while Hadley plays her family's recordings from distant Earth. She sits with me and I put my arms around her, thinking of the first time she played them for me. Hadley had explained that her family brought the stories as a way to remember the lands that they left behind, and the past that would always come with them.

The stories are ancient and I find them hard to understand. They describe endless expanses of water called oceans which I cannot imagine, and over them the man Odysseus travels in a vehicle called a boat. I do not know what the boat looks like, as these recordings have no images. I was born in Monopolis, just like my wife; raised to do my duty, not to imagine a different world.

I do enjoy listening to these old stories with her though. I like to hear about the one-eyed giant who tried to trap Odysseus, and how cleverly the man escaped the Sirens' luring song. Although he is seduced by a witch and a goddess, the story is about him trying to return to his wife. Each recording ends with a song, entreating anyone watching over us to protect us. I snuggle beside my wife on our couch and squeeze her hand in my own as we listen.

It took me a long time to find value in these stories. At first I could not see why she found them important. But over our years together, leaning closer in the evenings, I have discovered the reason. They have brought us together.

After the recording finishes, Hadley leans her head on my shoulder and, as usual, tells me her favourite stories, the other stories, the ones not in the recordings. She says that her grandmother whispered these Earth stories to her while she lay in her cot as a baby. When I ask how her grandmother knew the stories, Hadley says that they are passed from woman to woman in her family. I hear them for the first time from her.

She tells me that she wishes she could see a forest. She wants to see the trees and grass, flowers in all the colours from the stories. She wants to race through the homes of nymphs and dryads, calling them to dance and run with her. She wants to sing odes to the gods beneath a wide blue sky at the top of her voice.

I am not surprised. Hadley spends all her time in the gardens and complains often that they are not the bright and overwhelming places that she imagines in her stories. In these gardens, she must take time to dress in pressurised anti-contaminant gear before she can enter. She cannot dance there.

Hadley describes the tedious daily walk along rows of clumped leaves that grow in trays of liquified organics, recycled into fertiliser. She tells me that she once looked around carefully, side to side and behind her, even craning her head towards the high ceiling where heat lamps stare blindly. Seeing no-one to stop her, she unfastened one glove and then brushed a leaf with her bare skin. She smiles as she tells me of her indiscretion, shivering in delight at her bravado.

"It is truly something to raise a new life, Alex!"

I nod. I do not understand, but I can see the light in her eyes.

"I tend it every day, just like the others. But that one plant I seek out during my shifts. I check its nutrient levels most often. It is the one I watch to see if it is wilting."

My wife's eyes lose their focus. She is imagining a life with real children, instead of the plants that she gives her nurturing to instead. For me, it is enough to take care of the citizens in Monopolis. Each of us is responsible for the livelihood of the colony, and the same can be said for every citizen. We must all support each other, in order for the colony to survive.

It is my job to bring them back.

I reach over and place a hand on her knee.

"I'm sorry," I say, but she shakes her head and then focuses on my face. She smiles and places a hand on my cheek.

Then she tells me that we are all Odysseus, all of us here in Monopolis. She whispers in my ear that we have been captured, and must find our way out, find our way home. I tell her that there is no cyclops here, no great eye watching us. She closes her eyes and places a finger on my lips. I shake my head and try to explain to her that it is too dangerous to leave the colony, but I can see by the way she turns her head that she is not really listening. She looks through the walls of our apartment as though the ocean she must travel upon surrounds us.

But she has never left the walls, like I have, to bring back those who try to leave. She just says that people shouldn't be held this way.

I take her hands between my own, hold them close to my chest. I rub them with my thumbs, willing my thoughts into her. She has to understand why we all undertake our assigned roles, supporting one another against the danger that presses down from outside. She frowns. She hasn't seen the uncaring vastness. She doesn't realise how fragile Monopolis is. After eating dinner in silence, we retreat to bed and sleep with our backs to one another beneath a thin sheet.

In the morning, a high-pitched beeping cycles from beside our bed. The sound slips into my brain while I sleep, and I am already pulling on heavy work pants before I am fully awake. I am trained to respond to the alarm with speed and without question. The colony lights are still dim so I murmur a farewell towards our bed before tip-toeing out of the room. There has been a runaway. I will have to go outside the walls and retrieve them.

The lit walls in the hallway rise from darkness to dull orange, dotted by black camera lenses in each corner. I walk quickly past smooth doors, stepping around fellow citizens as they head out on their own errands. Some meet my gaze and look away. They see what lies beyond the Panoply reflected in my eyes. I pass my wrist over the door's scanner and step out into the broader vehicle hallways. A pair of Irini watch me walk down the ramp and wait for the stream of haulers in the lane to pause.

Sometimes I try to see past the thick protective visors to the faces of the Irini, wondering if my ex-colleagues are hidden behind them. Eventually, we all retire behind those tinted surfaces, but I am not ready to leave from my role yet. Someday when my mind has been filled by the void outside and I am no longer able to fulfil my purpose in the colony, perhaps. I detour towards the two figures in their heavy uniforms, holding my wrist out to theirs as I pass, to make sure they don't stop me. I must hurry, there has been a runaway.

IT IS my job to bring them back.

AT THE RETRIEVAL Depot the walls now glow a white that drives away all shadows. I join my team in the locker room, preparing to leave the safety of Monopolis. I pull on my suit to protect my weak human form from the radiation, and the cold. My boots have jagged soles, designed to let me walk across the surface, despite thick dust and slick ice. I finish by fastening my helmet in place, the visor polarised to protect my eyes.

Around me, the others are putting on the same uniform. We don't speak as we fasten bindings and tighten straps. Fear of what waits outside makes my muscles tense. I assume it is the same for the others. We do not talk about this moment, not even in the mandatory debriefings that follow each mission. But despite our fear, this job is vital; everyone has to support one another in this fragile colony. If any shirk their duty, the endless darkness outside is ready to crush us.

I climb onto the back of our six-wheeled retrieval vehicle, attach a carabiner to my perch and hook one heavy glove through a large metal loop. The glove is too thick to allow me to grip the loop. I watch the others do the same, features hidden by the heavy uniform we all wear.

Vibrations rumble where I am touching the crawler, up the soles of my feet and through my arm. They let me know that the engine has started, but I cannot hear it clearly. My suit fulfils its design, cutting me off from the world. My earpiece crackles as the others switch their transmitters on and we all check in.

"One."

"Two."

"Three."

"Four," I say.

"And Five in charge," finishes Hanaa. "Alright everyone, a breach in the Panoply was recorded six hours ago, while the night cycle was in process." We are so far from Sol, and the world rotates so slowly, that the first colonists decided to shield the city and run their own illumination cycles. They matched the human circadian rhythm as best they could, allowing the colonists to be more efficient.

"The breach was in the south wall, near the south gate," she continues, using the first colonists' traditional directions. "We will leave via that gate and try to pick up the trail."

"Is this a rescue?" asks Taylor, in a flat voice.

"Unknown," replies Hanaa. "It is unclear whether this runaway took anything with them."

Taylor's suited figure nods. It is the same answer that Hanaa gives to the same question before each mission. More often than not, we are Retrieval officers, locating the body and bringing it back into Monopolis for recycling. Every body's contribution to the support of the colony is vital.

"Have you ever been part of a rescue?" asks Justin. This is only the young man's second mission. Unease strains his voice.

With the comm open to everyone, it is unclear who he is asking. I stare at my glove, hooked around its metal loop. I know there are no medi-kits onboard.

"No," replies Hanaa. "I don't think any of us have."

I remember when we found a live runaway once, not long after I was assigned to the unit. One by one that team had been replaced as phobia swelled in their minds. Now I am the last one from that mission. I am the only one who remembers the runaway who stole a suit, rations, and even a mining rig. We pacified the runaway so we could get past the rig-lasers into their broken rock hideaway. Behind all that stone lay the rig, the rations, and their body. All those resources that the colony needed.

IT IS my job to bring them back.

THE CRAWLER RUMBLES out of the storage hanger and into the Agora. This massive hall is the largest space in Monopolis, lying beyond the labyrinth of halls, apartments, and offices. It is even bigger than the Stadium, with its blue LED ceiling, and carefully engineered faux-grasses. Citizens build strength and stamina in the Stadium, but in the Agora they meet and gossip and trade, building their minds. Men sell rations, women repair machines, citizens mend clothes. Children run between them all, past citizens speaking and dealing in their assigned booths. The council rooms are an imposing wall to the left of our depot.

I see angry faces in the Agora this morning. Drone-ship deliveries are becoming even more irregular. The traders have begun to raise their prices for foodstuffs and Earth-media. People grow hungry as they trade rations for a glimpse of a place that may no longer exist.

There is a commotion to my right and I turn my head. The helmet barely shifts and it is difficult to be sure what I see. The crowd in the Agora seems to have stepped away from a young man in dark clothes. A coiled snake is crudely sewn on the back of his jacket. Three of the Irini walk towards him, their hands raised in a calming gesture. Their protective suits are nearly as bulky as ours. I can't hear his yells, but I can see his red-faced anger.

The Irini reach him, grabbing his clothes in their fists. He twists and turns, and I can see that he must be shouting. He reaches out to pull at the uniform of the Irini who has him, but the protective suit is smooth. His fingers slip uselessly along the surface. Another Irini pulls out a metal rod and lifts it high. The crowd is already turning away, revulsion on their faces. Our crawler turns a corner and I lose sight of the man.

A wordless yell comes through the communicators, distorted and crackling in my earpiece. A figure has leapt onto our vehicle, wrapping arms around Hanaa at the front and trying to pull her aside. I hear Justin swear as another figure clambers up beside him.

A third person climbs up near me, his face so close that his breath fogs up my visor. His mouth is moving and his eyes drill into me, but I am sealed away from his fury in my uniform. I can pretend that he is no more than an irritation. I see the curled green snake embroidered by his collar as I push forward with my free hand, trusting the heavy bulk of my protective suit to help drive him away.

I can hear the muted grunts of the others as they do the same. The figures drop from the crawler, their already tattered clothing tearing further as they fall. A pair of dark Irini step forward. One grips a man by his loose shirt and heaves him up until his feet dangle over the pavement. The man's face is turning pale. Were they hoping we would be distracted by the first man in the Agora? Did they think the Irini would be spread too thin to help us? The second Irini salutes us on the crawler and waves us forward.

"I think that was Ellis," says Hanaa as the crawler rumbles into gear and moves forward, leaving the pile of people behind. "She always was a stickler for formalities like that salute. It's been so long." I remember how much time Hanaa used to spend with Ellis. The Irini keep to themselves. Their job is too important to allow fraternisation.

"I think there's been more activists recently," says Jess through my earpiece. "I heard one tried to break into the fertiliser plant. Claimed we shouldn't be recycling all the organics into growing new food!"

"Typical idiotic claim from these protestors. How could the colony survive if we don't grow food?" grumbles Taylor.

"At least the Irini didn't have to take that one far once they caught them," chuckles Jess.

"What do the protestors even want?" asks Justin. We ride silently through the Agora.

"That's not important," replies Hanaa eventually. I can't see her face behind the domed helmet, but I can imagine the way her face creases as she frowns. "They undermine the collective efforts we all undertake, unsettling Monopolis. Their actions are destructive towards the colony, and that is all we need to know. They step beyond the bounds of duty."

It is my job to bring them back.

"It's not fair on the rest of us," whines Taylor. "We follow the rules and make sure that the colony is functioning properly, and then they try to wreck it all. It's like they have no idea what we are all being protected from."

They probably don't, I think. None of us knew what was outside until we came on our first mission. I wonder how Justin felt when he first saw it, on his last mission. Maybe I should ask him.

The crawler enters a long long tunnel that hugs us so

tightly I could reach out and run my hand along the concrete surface as it races by. A series of automatic doors slide open to let us through, then snap shut again. I find myself holding my breath as we pass through each.

We pass the final doors and I hear Justin gasp. We are outside.

The void surrounds us as the crawler carries us out across broad icy plains. Clouds of dust lift impossibly slowly and settle like feathers in our wake. Even now, after many years and many missions, I feel the endlessness of it run fingers around my heart. Fear quickens my breath. A red alert flashes on my wrist before my helmet compensates.

As Hanaa drives us slowly away from the grey mountain that is Monopolis, I stare at the monochrome landscape of craters and cracked hills. They aren't as impressive as the massive features on Earth's moon that I was shown during training. No grey mountains claw at the black sky here, other than our colony. However, even that vast structure is shrunken and unimpressive when set into this broad world, flinching beneath a dark and endless sky.

The plain of dust stretches out to the bowed horizon, pocked by the evidence of meteors. Somehow the emptiness of the landscape makes the darkness worse. This world doesn't care enough to hate us. It will destroy us by accident, should we falter. The rubber wheels of the crawler leave a crisp trail across the ground as we begin our search.

The world our ancestors chose is cold and empty. I sometimes wonder why it was chosen. What possible reasons did they have to come to this place and decide to stay. Why would they ask their children and children's children to remain? But I cannot think this way. Questions like that create doubt and doubt is why there are runaways. The protestors are full of doubt, but all they bring is discord. They don't understand what we must work together to shelter from; the long flat plains of ice, the thick piles of dust, the dim grey surface. I won't weaken the colony.

We follow the standard search pattern, crossing back and forth on the pale plain, each of us watching the ground for evidence of the runaway. Though none of us speaks, I know that we are avoiding looking up into the limitless darkness that wraps over us. It is the night that we must keep from overwhelming Monopolis. That boundless threat is why we must all take on our roles without complaint. That is why we each support one another. That is why they cannot leave, taking with them precious resources and skills that the colony needs. But I have to leave the safety of the Panoply.

IT IS my job to bring them back.

IN THE SHELTER of a large crater we find her body, reaching out for something we can't see. Her suit was never intended to be worn for so long in these conditions, and it has ruptured, freezing her solid. She lies half buried in the powdered memories of asteroids.

I get off the crawler and stare up into the thick blackness that crowds us. I can feel it sucking away memories of warmth and brightness. I remember Hadley's recordings. This sky is the river Lethe, arched above us, and it tugs at the memory of life.

The others form a semi-circle around Hanaa where she is crouched over the runaway. They wait for me to step forward. Hanaa puts a hand on my shoulder. I look down at the body of my wife and bow my head.

The universe hangs all around, broken only by the smallest pinpoints of white; other worlds, distant stars above us. They are the only hope that I see, the only relief from the black. I imagine Hadley is reaching out to one of those stars, trying to reach out for Earth one last time. There is no way to tell if any of the tiny white dots in the sky are a connection from Earth or not. I hope that she found it anyway.

We are so distant here; the refreshing spray of the ocean in her stories was nothing against absolute zero. Here the stained glass colours of trees fade under the endless grey, black and white. We are too far for the nymphs and the dryads to welcome her soul and comfort her to their bosoms.

One of the others brings me the cadaver bag. I don't know which of the team it is through the dull golden shine of their visor, and they don't speak. White noise hisses in my ears like a theatre's roaring crowd, watching our chorus dance another tragedy. I step towards the outstretched hands lying below me and push them aside. I zip the bag around her, avoid those empty eyes; I trap her in the black plastic.

Over the horizon Charon rises. Uninvited stories of the ancient ferryman fill my thoughts, the one who took the dead away. I wonder if that skeletal ferryman watches us through the glowing blind eye of the twin-planet that fills the sky. Sweat runs down my back as I work on the exposed surface, beneath that ponderous gaze.

There are no glorious fields of green, no rolling meadows around us. There is nowhere for heroes to relive deeds that made them famous. Neither is there a Hades for them to moan in while they suffer. I have heard of other colonies that match those descriptions, floating around the titanic planets; Jupiter the king, Uranus the beginning. Colonies of beauty and wealth, where citizens take joy in every action. Still other colonies that must be wrought from the harsh world around them.

This is the third place, the nothing place, a grey place

where the dead remain still and wait for us to come and take them away. This is Pluto the Underworld and the outer worlds.

I remember Hadley's stories echoing in our apartment. Spoken memories of a place far distant. Fields and meadows and music and animals. A world that is brought out of death and decay thanks to six mere pomegranate seeds. A singer who tried to bring their dead wife home.

For a moment I hear a voice singing behind the buzz of my earpiece, singing one of the songs from my wife's recordings. I stare across the plain, to the small dome of Monopolis, oh so far away. The voice is soft and low, guiding another soul back towards the living. I realise it is my lips that shape this prayer. I turn back to the others as we stand awkwardly around the black bag. My song dwindles into the static as we lift together, grunts of effort passing through our communicators. I try to recall the face hidden inside the bag, but already she fades.

It wasn't the darkness we hide from that killed Hadley. It isn't the dangers beyond our city that wore her down. With our restrictions we asked her to take hemlock.

It is my job to bring them back.

The others lift her into place on the crawler as I watch. I am standing above the shape of her that remains in the dust. I crouch down and press two fingers into the soft ground where she sheltered, keeping her eyes on the pinpricks of respite in the sky. I leave two fresh craters, two obols, to pay her passage home.

DROUGHT

*It's been one month,
one week
and one day*

*since you
took our rain
away.*

*Your water-tank
dripping
echoes.*

*In your flower bed
untended roses
wilt.*

*A paddling pool
on the brown grass
unfilled.*

AARON DICK

I wait on the dusty
gravel driveway,
alone

since you disappeared
like a mirage
on the road.

The letter box
is empty
as the sky.

EELS BITE DEEP IN LAKE PUPUKE

Simon parked his car and looked out over Lake Pupuke. Bright reflections from the afternoon sun settling towards the horizon contrasted with the green lake waters. He didn't come here often anymore, but the memories he had made in his youth made him smile. Swans were scattered across the grass like abandoned white cotton balls, heads tucked low beneath wings, small black eyes staring out at the people walking down the concrete path.

The summer evening was warm and still. Small white puffs of cloud stretched through the sky overhead. Simon ran a hand through his hair as he followed the path, looking for Hazel. He spotted her leaning on the tree at the bottom of the slope, swiping through social media on her phone to pass the time.

"Hazel," he called as he drew closer.

She looked up and smiled, tucking her phone into the back pocket of her jeans. "Kia ora Simon!" She moved forward to meet him halfway and they gathered each other into a tight hug, kissing each other gently.

"Ooo," said Simon in surprise as the cool green stone of her necklace shocked him.

"Are you alright?" she laughed.

"I wasn't expecting that, it feels extra cold! Doesn't it shock you on a nice summer's day like this?"

She lifted a hand to the carefully carved piece. "I guess I just got used to it."

Simon squeezed her a little tighter. "Mmm, it's been so long since I've held you."

"It's been two days," she giggled.

"Long enough."

Simon was only half joking. He and Hazel had only been seeing each other for a few weeks since meeting behind the scenes at a Unitec play in Point Chev. Their connection had been the strongest that he had ever experienced. When they weren't having dinner, watching Netflix, or finding ways to go out in the evenings, his only thoughts were about how to enable those things to happen again as soon as possible.

"Have you been waiting long?" he asked.

"Not really," she replied. "Just long enough to wonder who brought the swans with them."

"What do you mean?" He turned to look at the birds scattered across the lawn. Now he could see that there were some geese amongst the swans, and plenty of ducks. They sat beneath the tall trees and Simon felt like they had always been there. His memories of coming to The Pumphouse certainly included them, as far back as he knew.

"They aren't native birds. They don't come from here, they are out of place. So who brought them?" Hazel's eyes narrowed slightly as she examined the creatures. "And what would it be like carrying a swan on a ship all the way from Europe!" she added.

Simon shuddered at the idea of trying to keep a bird as

unpredictable as swan on board a sailing ship for months. And why? The country was already full of so many varied and colourful species of bird, who had thought that what it needed was one more?

"I didn't know they weren't native," he admitted.

Hazel chuckled. "You thought they seemed natural enough paddling about the roto I suppose?" She squeezed his waist.

"Well, sort of. I mean, birds can migrate a long way, can't they?"

"Yeah, that's true. No, there used to be a native swan here in Aotearoa, a big black one. It was hunted to extinction unfortunately, I think."

"That's a shame. That's how you know these ones aren't native, huh?"

"Exactly."

"You know, when you brought this up, my first thought was why would someone have brought swans all that way?"

"Why would they have brought ferrets? Why would they have brought gorse?" scoffed Hazel. She smiled ruefully. "They probably thought they had a very good reason, but so much of what they brought ended up wrecking what was already here."

Near the edge of the lake a little girl in an olive and emerald jumper with long dangling sleeves was tearing apart some bread rolls and throwing them onto the grass for the birds. Brown sparrows flocked down to peck at the crumbs. A few swans lumbered to their feet and snatched at the pieces of bread, snapping their beaks to scare off the smaller birds. Then a large one reared up, beating its wide wings and lunging at the young child. Her mother rushed up to grab her, and her father lifted his arms and shouted, trying to scare the swan away.

"No matter who brought them, or why, I know that they are scary animals sometimes!" said Simon. "I remember coming to watch kids' plays here and they were just as bad then."

"There's only one way to cope with these sorts of displays," said Hazel, gripping his hand tightly and stepping forward. "We need to support that family."

"What?"

"The bird will back off if there's a crowd of us."

When they were halfway to the family, the bird squawked and backed away, tucking its wings into its sides and pretending that it had never been upset. The family smiled at Hazel and Simon and then led their child away.

"Come on," said Hazel. "The show isn't for another half hour. Let's get something to eat."

Next to the tree they had been standing under, at the end of the path and overlooking the tall reeds that grew up from the edge of the lake, was a French cafe. It was late but the shop was still open, so they walked inside. Simon was hoping that he would be able to get a beer, but he sighed when he realised that there only seemed to be very fancy coffee for sale.

"I might just get a flat white," he mumbled.

"I'll get a cola." Hazel gave her order to the young woman behind the counter, adding Simon's as well. "I like that neck-lace," she said, pointing out the curled green stone as delicate as cobweb against the server's neck. The young woman reached up and touched it with her fingertips then smiled at the compliment.

"Thank you. My brother carved it for my twenty-first birthday."

"You're very lucky," said Hazel. She and Simon made their way to a small round wrought iron table to wait for their drinks. The table had been freshly repainted in a deep green, though the chipped edges of the previous layer could be seen through it.

Hazel smiled as the waitress placed a tall glass and her bottle of cola on the table beside them, along with Simon's coffee.

She lifted the glass as she poured the fizzing drink into it.

"Have you ever noticed how cola is actually green?"

"What do you mean?"

"Usually people would say it's black, but it's really a very deep green."

"Show me," said Simon.

She held up the glass so that there was light glowing through from behind it. Simon could see how the thick dark liquid shone green where the light was strong enough.

"That's cool."

"I always thought so. Nice to know there's a bit of colour in the darkness."

"How does a French cafe end up here, on the shore of a massive lake in the suburbs of Auckland?" Simon said as he lifted his broad mug of coffee and sipped at it.

"Just like everything else, it's decoration, isn't it? The people who began to live here, who filled the place as though it was theirs, they didn't want it to be what it was. They needed something else. And so they brought along the things that they thought sounded luxurious from home. Mornings with coffee. Feeding the bright white birds who look so pretty as they drift along the surface of the water." Hazel sounded grumpy

Simon touched her hand. "Hey. Are you alright?"

She smiled. "Yeah, I just get caught up in my head sometimes, wondering how different the world could be."

"Let's go see the show, eh?"

They walked to the large red brick building beside the cafe: the Pumphouse Theatre.

"It was built to pump water from the lake to the homes in

the area," mentioned Hazel as they looked up at the tall square chimney. Simon nodded and led the way inside.

The middle-aged woman behind the counter checked their tickets and then a very young man with a bulbous adam's apple led them to their seats.

"Not sure that was really necessary," laughed Simon softly. "There's, what, a hundred seats in here? Did they think we'd get lost?"

"Shhhh," giggled Hazel.

Simon was looking forward to this. He had seen a flyer for the show stuck to a post near Unitec, where all the right sort of young theatre students might see it. It hadn't given much away, just the name of the play, some dates and times, and a review. "A true eye-opener" it had said, though Simon hadn't recognised the name of the critic. Phillip Howard, or something like that? He mentioned the play, A Golden Crown, to some of his friends, and they said that they had seen it before. Simon had been surprised.

"When did you get to see it?"

"Oh, recently, I think. Maybe a year ago?"

"A year ago! You didn't tell me?"

"Maybe it was last month?"

"You saw this run?"

"No. Maybe?"

It had been a strange conversation. When pressed, none of his friends had been able to give any more details, either about the contents of the play itself or when they had seen it. In any case, they had agreed with the reviewer, saying that the play had really made them consider some things that they hadn't thought of before.

And so Simon leaned forward as the lights dimmed and a figure stepped out onto the stage before him.

At first, Simon found it hard to understand what was

happening. There was no scenery, and the only hint of where the characters were was a large black cube set in the middle of the stage. At times it seemed to represent a castle in the distance, or a mountain that had to be scaled. The characters, clothed in plain black, spoke to one another about how they wanted more space in the land, and wished that the king would stop crushing anything that they tried to build. They agreed that perhaps the king did not understand, and that they would go to speak with him.

When the king entered he was dressed mostly in white, but small red and black geometric symbols had been placed on his sleeves and chest. He sat on the cube, which was now some sort of throne, and began a speech that despaired of the troubles that plagued his kingdom.

Simon nearly laughed. The speech explained that the king thought all his troubles were caused by the ungrateful and disruptive people who lived within his lands, the same people who had just rationally and calmly explained how they were living burdened by the king himself.

A golden crown lowered itself from above the stage until it hovered a foot over the king. *Wow, I can't even see the strings,* thought Simon. As he peered closer, trying to figure out this clever effect, he began to notice something strange from the corner of his eyes.

It was like an itch, if an itch was a sight and not a sensation. The vision crept forward from behind him, glowing brightly but also illuminating nothing else around him; a scratched line that coiled and jagged forward .

Simon turned his head to see what it was but the roof and seats looked normal. The rest of the audience was watching the show, their eyes reflecting pinpricks of light in the gloom. The white itch continued to creep forward along Simon's vision.

He blinked and looked down, lifting a hand to press against his eyes hard.

Hazel leaned over to place a hand over his, and whispered. "Is everything alright?"

"I'm just feeling a bit odd," murmured Simon back. Hazel gasped.

"What?" he asked, lifting his head to see what was wrong. His breath caught in his throat, and his mouth hung open.

There was a line of white light running along the outline of the stage now. Each edge of the cube was pierced by its glow, and the figures on stage seemed to be standing in front of a spotlight. The white aura beamed around them, bursting from above the seated king. And yet still the audience remained still and keen, paying rapt attention.

Simon glanced at Hazel, whose face seemed drawn.

"Can you see that?" he asked. She nodded, and then blinked and stared at him.

"You mean you can too?" she asked.

The glow began to stretch further along the stage and scenery, turning the room into a web of white lines and deep blackness, a colouring book in reverse. Simon felt his heart racing.

"How did they-"

The glow on stage brightened more and more, hiding any sign of the silhouetted cast. A shape remained, white and glowing and strong, filling the stage with its presence.

"As before, as I am, as it always will be," intoned a voice from the stage.

Simon felt his hands gripping the seat. His shoulders were tense and tight, but he could not look away from the presence that filled his vision.

"I am new here, though I am old, and you are part of me, as I am part of you," the voice tolled, as resonant as a massive church bell. The presence grew larger, pulsing with light. The many fractured lines in Simon's vision, that zig-zagged towards the thing, flared. It sat like a spider in the middle of a broken glass web, pulling everyone in the audience towards it.

"What do we do?" hissed Simon. Hazel was barely able to shake her head in response. She had no suggestions. *This can't be part of the show, what on earth is this?*

"I can feel some of you pulling away," the voice said. There was a hideous gurgling noise. Simon realised that the thing was laughing. Although it was impossible to see the true shape of whatever it was through the blinding light, Simon could tell that parts of it were pushing forward more than others. It was lopsided now, like uncooked dough rising, growing in thick clumps that tumbled forward and over the front rows of the audience.

"You can try little ones, but I am already in you. You brought me here. The Ides of March lifted me higher! You are my children and my parents. I will devastate you."

Simon felt tears rolling down his cheeks but he was still unable to move. He felt as though metal bands were wrapped around his body, keeping him constrained to his seat. He managed to push his little finger over far enough to feel Hazel's hand, and she extended her own. Fingers hooked together they faced the oncoming thing.

It swelled in glutinous curves that nauseated Simon. The thing seemed to be growing outside any recognisable world that Simon knew, at once larger than a skyscraper but still contained within the small theatre. He could not turn away.

As it passed over the rows in front of them, Simon could see the audience members inside it. They were shadows that quickly vanished in the white light, as though they were evaporating or burning away. There was no noise or movement from any of them.

"Simon," said Hazel. Her voice sounded as though she was shouting from the end of a tunnel; echoey and faint. He tried to turn to look at her but couldn't, and so he tried to squeeze her finger with his own to show that he had heard her. "Stay with me Simon."

"Goodbye silly children." said the voice. Simon focused on the feeling of Hazel's fingers and the memory of the way she had kissed him under the tree outside, and then the glowing thing washed over them both.

Simon heard the applause of the audience and shook his head. All around him, the audience was standing and clapping as hard as they could. He turned and saw Hazel sitting next to him, looking just as confused as he was.

Slowly, not wanting to draw attention to himself, he stood and joined in the clapping. As he brought his hands together, he looked around the theatre. The house lights were raised now, and there was a row of figures on stage bowing and waving to acknowledge the applause.

Simon leaned over to Hazel.

"Did you see that?" he asked. He couldn't believe his own recent memory, he must have been hallucinating.

"I certainly did. But the thing that interests me is that you saw it."

"What?" Simon glanced at her. Her face was drawn and she looked exhausted, but there was a sparkle in her eye as she looked at him.

"Not everyone notices it. Most people walk on by and never acknowledge it. But I've seen it every day of my life."

"You've seen that thing every day?" Simon was shocked. How could she function with such a monstrosity interrupting her life? He felt as though he had been hit in the stomach with a bat. He couldn't think clearly. Where had the thing gone? Had it ever truly been there?

"It doesn't look like that most of the time," she said. She nudged him with her elbow, to start leaving their seats before the rest of the audience. "Come on, let's get out of here."

They managed to get out of their row and start walking towards the exit. They weren't alone, though most of the audience was still clapping. One of the others moving towards the exit met Simon's eyes, and he recognised their confusion. He was feeling it himself.

Simon tried to process what he had seen. What was it? Why had barely anyone noticed? What did Hazel mean that it didn't usually look like that? What had he actually seen and how come it hadn't had any effect on the theatre?

Outside, night had fallen. The lake lay black and deep in front of the Pumphouse. The world was dusted with light from the stars overhead and the houses around the lake, reflected by waves on its surface. Hazel held Simon's hand and led him past the cafe back to the single tall tree at the bottom of the slope beneath the carpark.

He stopped her in the lee of that tree and turned her to face him.

"What was it?" he asked. He could hear the crack in his voice as he tried to keep himself under control. He had to know what she meant. The glowing thing couldn't be really real. Not when the world seemed so quiet and still and cool as they stood beneath the tree, beside the lake.

"I don't really know, but I know I've seen that light all my life. It traces the world, cars, buildings, people. Sometimes it erupts and some horrible thing spreads out just like what happened in that theatre."

"You see it in the whole world?" He glanced around but saw nothing. "Can you see it now?"

"No, it doesn't really show up in nature. That's why I live in the Waitakeres." She shook her head and sighed. "It's always terrifying, but I've figured out ways to let it pass over me without hurting too much."

"I can't believe what you're telling me. You mean that you are used to moments like that? And you just, I don't know, you just ignore it?" He felt as though every part of his skin was itching, just at the thought of ignoring that thing as it swallowed him up, over and over.

"I know." She shrugged. "But if you experienced that every day, tell me how would you cope? Sometimes I try to fight it, but it's exhausting."

Simon had to stop questioning her as the audience from the theatre began to catch up with them. The murmur of their conversation came with them, chattering like a flock of birds. Simon found it off-putting. How could these people not have noticed? Was he imagining things? But Hazel saw it everywhere. Were they both losing their minds?

Simon stepped closer to Hazel and put his arm around her waist. His heart rate slowed as he felt steadied by her presence. He would stand next to her and they would face whatever it was, together.

As the first people in the crowd approached, Simon looked at them. Their eyes shone with a light that was brighter than any reflection should be in the dark night. He stepped closer to Hazel as the crowds walked by, white teeth flashing in their mouths. He thought that he could hear bells tolling beneath their footsteps.

The waters of Lake Pupuke swirled, deep and dark and old.

ECHO

A paper-white butterfly
flew into my lips
and felt like my daughter's kiss.

In that moment
it didn't matter
where we were.

THE VERY YOUNG GIRL

ORIGINALLY PUBLISHED IN ES WAR EINMAL GRIM(M) FAIRY TALES FOR AOTEAROA NEW ZEALAND

Once upon a time there was a very young girl who was scared to dream. Every night in her dreams she fell through the air, while shadowed figures with glowing eyes reached out to pull her away into the dark unknown. She would start awake from these dreams, then toss and turn until morning, hoping the shadows would leave her be. This night she lay in her sleeping bag, staring at the roof of her tent as her father's snores drifted from his. Her breath misted above her face in the dark cold air. Her heart would not be still. She rose from her tent, to walk through the leafy trees and dirt paths of the nearby bush until she grew tired.

Branches loomed over her in darkness. She was wary of the shadows that clustered beneath the trunks, thinking of the watchers in her dreams. She told herself 'They are only dreams' but the breeze's cool touch on the back of her neck made her shiver. Soon the chill night air made her skin damp. She longed to return to her tent, but discovered the paths through the bush had tricked her and now she was lost. She sat down beside a small waterfall and cried into her hands, fearful that she would never find her way back.

The leaves beside her rustled and the very young girl looked up. There stood a possum, watching her with his small green eyes. He smiled through smoky fur and asked "Why do you cry, child?"

"I have become lost in this bush," replied the girl, hurriedly wiping tears from her cheeks. "The darkness scares me, I am cold, and I will never see my family again."

"Do not be upset," said the possum, stepping backwards towards the trees that surrounded the pool. "I know the way back to your campsite. If you make me one promise, I will return you to your father." His fur hid him between the shadows and bark. Only his green eyes were to be seen.

"Anything." The girl rose and stepped closer, clasping her hands together.

"You must promise to hold onto something for me, and to hold it tight until I tell you to stop. Will you promise?"

The girl could see the possum's paws were empty and there was nothing with him for her to hold. She bit her lip and paused. But dew was trickling down her neck, the darkness pressed all around, she desperately wished to be in her tent, and so she said, "I promise."

"Excellent!" The possum beckoned her down one path and led her through the bush. Flashes of moonlight speared through the leaves, lighting her way as she followed. Soon she was crossing the small grass clearing towards her tent.

"I shall call upon you to keep that promise," said the possum from behind her, but when she turned to thank him he had gone.

· · ·

BY THE NEXT morning the very young girl had forgotten her promise and her dreams. She enjoyed breakfast with her father then ran to explore a nearby beach while the sun was strong. While walking between flax bushes, she thought she saw smoky fur in the long grass on the sand dunes. As she walked closer she remembered her promise. She passed an old wooden sign on a thin post and began searching through the grass. Waves crashed noisily on the sand, reflecting light into her eyes, making it difficult to find anything.

All of a sudden, a brown bird burst from the grass and sand, flapping its wings in her face. The bird cawed and screeched as the girl cried out in surprise and fell to the ground. A second bird, with white feathers on its chest, joined the first and together they pummelled the girl with their wings and scratched at her with their claws.

"Please stop," cried out the girl, hiding her head beneath bleeding arms. "What have I done?"

"You are running through our home," replied the first bird, with a voice sharp as its beak. "If you don't turn back, you will surely crush our eggs." The white-chested bird continued beating the poor young girl with its wings.

"I'm sorry, I didn't know. If you will stop attacking me, I will gladly make amends somehow."

The white-chested bird paused and tilted its head to stare at the girl. "We have little time to find food for ourselves. Do you swear to watch our eggs safely if we leave?"

The girl nodded. "I myself dream of being taken away in my sleep. I will keep watch so your eggs may rest peacefully. I swear it by my parents."

The birds were satisfied by this, and showed the very young girl their nest. Three small eggs sat in the sand beneath a clump of grass. They left her to watch the eggs and swooped along the beach, vanishing over the headlands. The girl sat down near the nest and waited. The sun slipped behind the clouds and the world grew dim.

TIME PASSED, as it passes, until the girl noticed a movement in the grass and a flash of dark fur. It was a rat, creeping through the dunes. The rat smiled at her with its large teeth, and moved towards the nest. The girl felt scared of its cold teeth and eyes, but she remembered her promise to the birds so she stomped and shouted and drove the rat away.

Little by little, a cat came slinking along the dunes. The cat had seen the eggs in the nest and was smarter than the rat. It tried to hide in the shadows, and slip past the girl, but she was determined to keep her word and had kept a keen watch. She saw the cat and threw a stone, striking it on the side so hard it yowled and ran away.

AT LAST SHE heard the sound of something walking through the sand. She turned and saw the possum standing behind her, smiling with his small sharp teeth. His smile spread through his spiky grey fur, wider and wider as he reached forward to touch her shoulder.

"Hello my dear," he said, his green eyes glancing past her at the nest. "I have come to claim my promise." The very young girl shied away from his snuffling pink nose.

"Of course, I gave you my word. But I have also promised to help these birds protect their nest."

The possum's tongue slicked across his thin lips. "I know these birds. I had thought they would fly away when you crashed through the grass, not make you promise to watch their nest. No matter, you promised me first after all. Come, I will show you what you must hold."

The very young girl knew she must keep her promises. Regretfully she followed the possum to the edge of the dune, where he pointed at the worn old sign post that jutted from the grass. The sign was faded, but the girl saw now that it warned people to be careful of the endangered birds nesting in the dunes. She held onto the thin post, feeling the harsh wood against her soft palm.

"Remember, you promised to hold on until I tell you to stop." With those words the possum turned back into the dunes with hunger in his green eyes.

The very young girl watched him leave, pushing long grass aside with his furry arms. She despaired for the eggs, unprotected now from the possum, who she realised had tricked her into crossing the dunes. She needed a way to keep both her promises at once. Though scared of the possum's sharp teeth, claws and green eyes, she summoned her strength and pulled on the post, lifting it from the ground. Though it strained her arms she held on to it, just as she had promised, and followed the possum.

She caught up with the possum as he reached into the nest, and swung the post with all her strength, delivering a mighty blow to his head. The possum screamed and fell to the ground, where she managed to strike him again. He raised his arms and yelled "Stop!" before she could hit him further. As soon as he spoke the girl's promise was kept, and she dropped the post on top of him. He pushed it aside and ran from the dunes, disappearing into the bush.

THE GIRL CONTINUED to watch the nest for the rest of the day, facing down cold wind and dark shadows. The birds returned, thankful for her help and praised her for saving their eggs from the deceitful possum. That night when the very young girl curled into her sleeping bag she was no longer afraid. In her hand she clutched a feather from the birds. As she slept, she no longer fell. Now she flew, diving towards the shadows and driving them away with her beak and wings. The very young girl dreamed.

THE WORLD IS GONE IN EACH NIGHT'S CHILL

This shrouded morning
I will leave off my dressing gown
and leave you with your dreams,
clutching my pillow.

I will watch the mist outside
that hides us inside
as my skin goosepimples.

I will step over your bag
and tell myself, again,
to get a side table for you.

I will boil the kettle
under the just rising sun,
its rays frosted by the mist
and, with my breath clouding,
I will make tea in chipped mugs.

Together we will sit,
sipping our hot drinks,
and watch the encroaching day
burn our mist away.

SURFACING

ORIGINALLY PUBLISHED IN CHILDREN OF
THE DEAD: LOST LULLABIES

Zahra ran down the beach's damp sand. Her father was pulling a small dinghy into the waves lapping the ocean's edge. White paint flaked off its sides.

"I want to come too," she yelled, waving a hand over her head.

"What?" Her father straightened up to look at her, and then shaded his eyes to peer past her to the little bach they were holidaying in.

Zahra laughed and jumped up into her father's arms. He clutched at her, keeping her from dropping back down onto the sand.

"Did you ask your mother?" he said slowly as he lowered her back down.

"No, I haven't seen her this morning, but she'd probably yell at you," laughed Zahra. "She doesn't like it when I do things the same way you do."

Her father reached out and ruffled the soft brown hair on her head.

"She loves everything you do, chicken." He sighed and scrubbed a hand across the rough hair on his chin. "Have you put on sunscreen? Have you been to the toilet?"

Zahra nodded and jumped up and down with excitement.

"It's probably better if you're with me anyway. Climb in."

Zahra squealed as she clambered in and sat on a cross-plank. Her father shoved the dinghy into the water, and it bounced over the small waves. Zahra grabbed the side and giggled as her heart jumped up towards her throat.

"Careful chicken!" called her father. Then he threw himself into the dinghy, where he sprawled in the hull in front of Zahra. He pulled himself upright and moved to sit by the outboard motor clamped onto the stern. A black rubbish bag was stuffed beside him. Each wave shifted the dinghy a little closer to the sand.

"Quickly dad!" yelped Zahra.

He tugged at the motor's rope, yanking the plastic handle three times before the motor finally coughed and the propeller spun in a noisy blur. Zahra's father lowered the prop into the sea, and a warble of bubbles accompanied them as they nosed out into deeper water.

Zahra leaned forward, relishing the salty spray that dampened her face. Pale cliffs on either side of the bay slipped away behind her. She reached down to let her fingers bounce and break through the ocean's glassy green surface. The sun warmed her back.

Zahra was so happy to be out on the ocean with her father. It was quiet out here with only the two of them, even with the motor's grumble. Her father sat silently with one hand on the tiller, guiding them past small waves that crashed over half-submerged rocks, until they reached the middle of the bay. The slow swell dropped away under the boat, lifting Zahra's heart again, and she smiled.

Distant seagull cries barely reached across the water, as faint as memories; like the shouts that kept her up at night until her eyes felt like they were burning. The swell lifted the dinghy and her stomach dropped. But right now the sea breeze was cool and the air was still, and her eyes felt clear.

Her father turned off the motor and they drifted in the current. The swell slapped against the boat's wooden sides like someone knocking at a door. Zahra laughed at the thought someone could be coming up from the depths below her feet.

"Not right now," she said, looking down at the wooden hull. "Dad and I are busy at the moment."

Zahra's father laughed. She was so happy to see him smile at her joke. That smile was bright and wide, and always so welcome when he finally let it out from behind his scratchy beard.

"Are you ready for some fishing?" he asked.

"Not yet! Can I go for a swim first?"

He chuckled and rolled his eyes dramatically. "Again? Alright, I suppose you can."

Zahra barely waited for him to finish before she pulled her tee shirt off and threw it down. Then she moved along the dinghy, trying not to set it rocking, and dove into the dark water.

Below her feet she saw the ocean stretch away, cold and deep. Zahra held her breath and looked down, enjoying the way she kicked slowly to keep herself afloat while beams of light speared down into the emptiness. Her heart felt like it was floating higher in the water.

The sea was filled with tiny flecks that drifted and swirled around her. The thumps on the boat sounded louder here, in the water. Zahra wondered if anything else swam in this bay. She couldn't see anything below her.

Zahra pushed up through the surface and gasped in a deep breath.

"Are you okay?" called her father. He had lifted the fishing rods and was fiddling with their lines.

"I'm fine! Watch this!" Zahra pulled herself forward and down, diving under the dinghy and twisting as she went. Cold water pressed around her shoulders and she placed a hand on the boat's underside as she swam below it. The wood felt rough on her palm. Behind her head, the ocean was quiet.

On the far side, Zahra burst out of the water again with a loud splash.

"Well done chicken!" said her father from the other side of the boat. He scooped up a handful of water and washed his hands as he moved to her side. "It was you knocking on the boat, was it?"

"No!" she giggled, shaking water from her face.

"Oh no? Then who was it?"

"I don't know, there's nothing down there!"

"I hope there's something there, or we're going to waste a lot of time with these!" He hoisted two thin black fishing rods up so that Zahra could see them clearly.

Her father hauled her back into the dinghy which made her stomach drop, then Zahra sat with the fishing rod in her hands as the sun dried her. Her father chopped red meat into small cubes on a plastic chopping board he had set on top of a blue chilly bin. Zahra tried to fit them onto her hook, but her small fingers found the bits of meat too slippery. Her father reached out without speaking and took the bait from her. He hooked the bait and then handed it back. She smiled her thanks and then dropped the bait into the water.

Together they sat silently, watching the ends of their rods, and the thin lines that plunged down from them. Zahra's heart lifted as swell dipped the dinghy, sunlight glinting off the water. In the distance, the land was green and bright.

Zahra's thoughts drifted to when she and her parents had arrived at the bach. The driveway to the small cabin was steep and rain had left the dirt track slick with mud. The car had been flooded by the engine's roar and the spatter of wheels skidding, but it was their angry voices that had made her cover her ears. The car had bumped wildly as her father tried to control it, making her stomach drop and leaving her feeling nauseous.

The thoughts faded before Zahra had to recall her mother's furious glare at her father, or remember her voice curdled with anger. Instead, Zahra lifted her face and closed her eyes. She let the sun's warmth spread over her skin, leaving her feeling clean, patches of drying salt constricting on her shoulders. She sucked in a deep breath and then opened her eyes again.

After she and her father had sent a dozen pieces of bait into the water, Zahra noticed something.

"Dad, what's that?"

"Where?"

Zahra pointed past her line, to a small black shape sticking up from the water. The ocean's surface spread out from it like smooth green glass.

"Probably a shark, attracted to-"

"A shark!" shrieked Zahra before he finished. She pushed herself across the boat, trying to move as far from the object in the water as she could. Her father placed a comforting hand on her shoulder.

"It's okay, that's only a little one. We're safe and sound here in the boat."

Together they watched the fin slide closer to the boat. As it approached, Zahra noticed a second object behind the first. *It's the shark's tail,* she realised. She watched the shark draw alongside the boat. It was a hammerhead, the same length as her leg.

"Wow," she breathed.

"We haven't had much luck so far," muttered her father. "Let's see if I can catch this at least."

"What do you mean?" asked Zahra, but he was too busy rummaging between the oars that lay along the bottom of the boat. He pulled out a grey aluminium pole with a massive hook on the end.

"I'll see if I can gaff the thing as it goes by." He peered over the side, his fist tight around the gaff.

"Be careful! What if it bites you?"

"I'll be fine. You just have to watch them, so they can't turn on you."

Zahra watched as the small black fin swam alongside the boat until it was directly beneath her father. He lunged the gaff into the water and then yanked it back. The shining metal hook held nothing.

"Damn. It went under the boat."

Just like I did, thought Zahra.

"I'll get it on the other side," her father said, and he stepped quickly across the dinghy. It lurched as his weight shifted, and Zahra's stomach dropped. He stabbed the gaff back into the water but she saw the fin swim away from the boat.

"Damn it!" snapped her father. "Why does nothing ever go my way? I just want to catch some blasted fish!" The shark swam in a tight circle, a few metres further from the boat than he could reach with the gaff.

Zahra shrank back from his rough voice and ducked her head, closing her eyes.

"I'm sorry," she whispered. She steeled herself, then

opened her eyes to watch his response. The fins in the water beyond him dove, vanishing from sight.

He snorted and dropped the gaff back onto the oars with a loud clatter. "Ah, I can't really blame you. Come on. Let's see if that shark left any other fish down there for us."

Zahra sat while her father prepared her hook for her. The sun was drifting behind bands of cloud now. The sea's surface darkened, no longer reflecting bright white sunlight. The water was as smooth and dark as a marble floor. Zahra resisted the impulse to jump out and run along that floor. The land across it looked too far away.

Zahra's memories stirred as she sat in the quiet. Voices from last night. How she had kept her focus on the plate of peas and boiled carrot in front of her, while they shouted from either side. How he had stormed out in a rage, into the darkness outside the bach. The crash of the door slamming behind him. Zahra had risked looking up. Her mother's hard face had stared back.

"You'll need to be in bed when he gets back, with that mood on him. It's dark out there," her mother had declared. Zahra had gulped down the last mouthfuls of dinner, though it made her nauseous, then rushed to her bed. She had burrowed beneath her blanket; warm, surrounded, hidden. It was dark out there. The front door had banged open.

A gust of wind made Zahra shiver. Her father pulled in his line again.

"Blast. Baited again. What on earth is down there?" He glared at the ocean.

Zahra didn't reply.

"Something's eating all our bait, I can see that." He balled his hand into a fist. "Taking everything that we're sending down there. No matter what I do, they just take, take, take!" He kicked at the boat's side. The thud echoed more than Zahra would have expected.

"Maybe we should go back now?" she asked quietly. "Before whatever is eating the bait knocks on the hull again?"

"No. I'm going to catch something." Her father ignored her joke. His eyes were hard and as dark as the sea. Zahra wondered what could have been swimming below them, picking their hooks clean without a twitch on the line.

The wind brought more clouds. Zahra pulled her tee shirt back on, but the thin material wasn't enough to stop her skin rising into goose-pimples. She watched some seagulls fly away, until they were only dots in the sky, then were gone. The clouds felt close, as though they were gathering into piles that pressed down towards where she and her father sat alone in their tiny boat on a wide and empty sea.

Zahra turned her attention away from the rod in her hands and looked towards where her mother waited in the bach. Grey mist hid the distant beach, a thin curtain that was drawing along the headlands. She wondered if it was rain, coming to soak her and her father.

There was a tug on her line.

"I think I caught something!" she yelped in surprise. The end of her rod bent sharply down towards the surface. The reel whined as string was pulled from it. The rain was still approaching.

"Wind it in, wind it in!" cried her father. He stretched out a hand, as though he would yank the rod from her grip. "We're running out of time!"

Zahra leaned away from him and wound the handle as hard as she could. The line screamed, and the rod pulled so hard that she was sure it would snap. The patter of rain on the ocean grew louder, and ripples spread across the glassy surface.

"Stop, stop!" her father yelled. "Something's wrong!"

Zahra paused and held as still as she could. Her father shifted along the dinghy and took the rod from her. He lifted it, and watched as the end ducked lower. Then he pushed the rod down, and Zahra heard him groan as the rod's end lifted up.

"You've snagged the line," he snapped. Rain plastered his hair to his skull. Zahra wiped water away from her eyes. She lowered her head.

Rain soaked their clothes as Zahra watched her father try to yank the line free over and over again. He started the motor to move the dinghy towards the snag, but it didn't free the line. Zahra watched rainwater start pooling in the hull and wondered how deep the puddle could get before they would be in danger of sinking.

"It's no good," snarled her father. "You've ruined it."

He reached down to a black plastic box that sat next to the chilly bin. When his hand came back up, it held a long curved knife. "That was a good one, and you've wasted it," he muttered as he took the knife and held its edge to Zahra's line. There was a sound like a rubber band breaking, and then the rod snapped back to its usual shape. He thrust the rod back to Zahra and then tossed the knife into the puddle.

"I should have expected you would cause trouble, and now you've kept us out in this rain so long that we're soaked, cold, and taking on water! What do you have to say for yourself?"

Zahra knew better than to answer.

"I'm done with this." He started the motor again and guided the dinghy in a wide circle. He wiped water from his face with the back of his wrist. The rain was close around them, and Zahra could no longer see the headlands. They drifted on water that was peppered with ripples. The sea was dark below them. "There's no other way to go now."

Zahra's father hunched next to the puttering motor, its

rumble muffled by the rain, his face turned away as he looked for any sign of something through the drizzle. Zahra felt the hull lift beneath her feet, and her stomach dropped. A web of thin dark strands hung down from the chilly bin's lid, stuck to its side. The boat moved higher, rising on a mound of water that reflected nothing from the heavy clouds overhead. The rubbish bag at her father's feet was flat and empty. The knife splashed in the water between them. He met her eyes. There was darkness below and all around, and it rose higher.

BUTTERFLIES DANCE LIKE MOUNTAINS

1. "REMEMBER"

The young boy, whose name means the thin frost on puddles during autumn mornings, spoke to his grandmother, whose name means the yearning of a tree towards the sky.

"Mother asked me to hunt some redbeaks who waddle through shallow water. We are going to make a meal for our neighbours River and Gravel tonight, to thank them for their help looking after Ray while she was unwell. Mother said to ask you how to get to the best place to hunt for Waddling Redbeaks?"

His Grandmother Sky smiled and nodded. Frost's younger sister, whose name means a clear ray of sunshine splitting the clouds, had been ill recently and the neighbours had nursed her when Frost's parents could not stay home. Grandmother Sky's thin fingers moved ceaselessly, weaving the rushes she had gathered that morning into a broad basket.

"Waddling Redbeaks make fine meals and you will be able to snare some of them in the grove that Tide created when he brought water from Sleeping Mountain." She smiled at him over the rushes she was weaving. "You remember the story of Tide finding the water in the mountain, yes?"

Frost nodded. The story of his great-father, whose name means the strength of the rising tide, travelling through the land in order to find water pure enough to clean the stars was one of his favourites. Grandmother Sky smiled, but repeated parts of the story to him anyway.

"To find Spring Grove you must pass through the forest where the trees swarm around one another, where Tide showed that he was not too proud to bend. Your father has taught you how to reach the far end of its path safely. Remember that the trees are not cruel or kind, they have their own reasons and it is their own place.

Beyond Swarming Forest you will find the place where the boulders swim. I know you have played there many times. Instead of playing among the boulders, you will need to climb until you find the place where Tide leapt into the sky alongside the rocks, the place where they breach and take in the wind.

Then you will find yourself walking the ridge that marks Sleeping Mountain. Along the ridge you will need to be careful of the earth rolling over. The mountain sleeps uneasily, and many people have been crushed as gnats by the mountain's agitation. Have you walked the ridge before?"

Frost shook his head. He had spent many days following his father through Swarming Forest and he had shining memories of the days he had been allowed to play where the boulders swim, but he had been warned not to climb to the ridgeline.

"Then you must step slowly and listen to the voice of the mountain. Tide sang the mountain to sleep but it may push you aside, as we push aside an insect walking on our arm when we sleep. You will see Tide's song in the hills and valleys that surround Sleeping Mountain. Be sure to watch the song closely for signs that the mountain wakes.

Follow the ridge to its highest point and you will see a valley on the far side of the mountain that sleeps. That high point is where you will leave thanks for the mountain's quiet.

That valley is wide and green. Where it meets Sleeping Mountain you will find a grove of trees with spiked leaves that grow deep red fruit. Waddling Redbeaks often nest there, near the spring that Tide struck from the side of the mountain. While you are there, you should drink the water. After all," Grandmother Sky smiled at Frost. "The water is pure enough to clean the stars.

Hunt only enough Waddling Redbeaks for the meal tonight. Taking more would scare them away." Frost's grandmother continued weaving as she recounted the path to him. He nodded and recited the path back to her.

"Good lad. Make sure to bring thanks with you."

Frost nodded. "I will look in the gourds for some food for Sleeping Mountain."

He kissed his grandmother on the cheek and gathered up his carry bag. Grandmother Sky had woven it for him many years earlier, out of rushes taken from the river that curls through the fields near where it emptied into the bay that provides life. The bag was dark and light in a regular alternating pattern, and he loved it. Into the bag he tucked a snare he had tied during a rainy day and then went outside.

Frost opened the gourds hanging along the edge of the roof. Inside each was stored a small amount of dried fish, caught by Ray and Frost when they went out in Providing Bay on their boat. Then he picked up a little gourd that he could fill with fresh water, and jammed the cap back on to keep it safe. The gourds had all been carved with flowing decoration by his mother, whose name meant the sound of a Calling Curved-Beak. Ray came to the doorway and watched him.

"Are you feeling better Ray?" he asked his sister.

"Better, yes," she nodded. "Thanks to our people." She made a small gesture that included all the homes nearby, representing all the people who were part of the village that was home. "But not well enough to come with you."

Frost laughed kindly. "I don't believe mother or father would approve of your climbing Sleeping Mountain and walking their spine with me. It sounds very dangerous."

Ray snorted. "As if you understand the difference between danger and safety. Take care Frost." They waved to one another as Frost walked away between the buildings of Home.

He walked towards Swarming Forest, far beyond the grassy fields and cultivated gardens that surrounded Home. Other friends and family raised their hands to him as he passed by, taking the chance to rest their backs and arms from the labour of weeding and harvesting and planting.

The sun had time to rise three fingers further into the sky before Frost walked among branches that shifted without pausing, through a path that was sometimes hidden by slim trunks that jabbed to the sky. Thick twisted stumps rumbled past, but stayed clear of the path. The keepers would herd away wandering trees, to stop them causing problems for those who walked the forest. Frost knew that the keepers were less protective of anyone who left the path.

A keeper was out in the trees now, waving at Frost, who waved a hand in reply. Leaves and thin twigs immediately stretched down to caress his hand and he laughed as they tickled him. The trees rustled as they slipped around him, tracing along his skin with needle leaves. He pulled his hand away, and the thin tips of the branches leaned down further, scratching at his cheek.

"Settle down, settle down," laughed a second keeper, who came stepping along the branches towards Frost. It was his father, whose name means the sound of thunder far away.

"Good morning son," Thunder said as a broad branch lowered him to stand on the path by his boy.

"Good morning."

"What brings you here today?"

"Mother needs something for dinner tonight, because we are thanking River and Gravel for their care of Ray. Grandmother suggested I go to Spring Grove behind Sleeping Mountain to snare some Waddling Redbeaks."

"That sounds like an excellent idea, but it is a long way from here. You haven't been there before, have you?"

Frost shook his head. Thunder frowned and scratched the back of his neck.

"Then you will need to take care. The place where boulders swim is known to you but the ridge of Sleeping Mountain can be dangerous. You have never walked the mountain's spine before." He reached over and placed a hand on Frost's shoulder. "Be polite to the mountain. You are a good boy, and I do not think they will be angry at you." Thunder's deep dark eyes were serious. Frost knew that his father was worried. He also knew that his father had faith in Frost's ability to behave correctly.

"I will. Grandmother suggested that I bring thanks with me for the mountain, so I got some dried fish." He lifted the handful of fish he had brought with him to show his father.

Thunder hummed. "That is a good idea, but I think you should be more generous with Sleeping Mountain. Here." He pulled a package out of the bag that was slung over his shoulder. It was wrapped in a broad soft leaf. "Take one of my flatcakes. They are sweet, and I have found that Sleeping Mountain enjoys sweet things."

Frost thought of what his younger sister would say if she were with them. Ray always disliked taking things from others, or possibly leaving them without something that they needed. It had led to some odd arguments between himself and his sister, as she tried to refuse offers from their friends and neighbours when they played with the other youth in the village. Frost would insist that the village only survived because everyone was willing to help one another, and Ray would certainly offer what she could to others; but still she found it difficult to accept what was given. Frost was willing to share in both directions however. He took the package from his father.

"I will make do with some berries today," Thunder said. He turned to the shifting trees beside him and whistled a request. A branch lowered and unfurled a leaf, revealing a small bunch of dark glistening purple fruit. Thunder held out his hand, palm facing the branch and murmured "I am Thunder of Home. You know me. I seek some food." There was a shiver through the vine and then the tall man plucked the fruit from the vine and tucked it into his bag. Then he placed his hands at his sides and bowed. Frost watched his father's movement carefully.

"You can have this dried fish as well," he suggested, but Thunder smiled and waved him on along the path.

The young boy continued through Swarming Forest. Sometimes he had to wait on the path as trunks shifted over it. He knew that leaving the path to walk around those trunks was dangerous. Although the keepers managed the forest well, all the villagers knew that the forest was its own creature that lived alongside people, and to leave the path was to submit yourself to that creature. The creature was untame and could turn easily, without thought, without malice. Frost walked on the path until he reached the end of the forest and found the first ripples of the place where the boulders swam.

II. "THE PATH"

The grassy sides of the hills shifted as slowly as clouds, like waves on the sides of a pond; giant ripples that drifted down from the heights towards him. The wind danced along these mounds and swirled around Frost's face, catching at his hair. Broad fields of grass stretched away beside him, shimmering in that wind, and full of delicate blue butterflies, whose name meant the song Tide sang to calm the mountain. They jagged from one small white flower to another. Frost smiled and watched the hills until he spotted a school of boulders leaping from peak to peak.

Carefully he moved up the hill, half climbing and half walking on its gently shifting surface, until he approached the large rocks. The grass sank below his feet, carrying him lower and lower, until he felt it bob and began to rise once more.

The nearby boulders were a variety of colours, pale and smooth, dark and cracked, speckled and rough. He knew that the rocks saw him, because they began to settle and move around the peak of the hill until he was surrounded by their forms, the smaller rocks hidden behind the bigger ones. He reached out a hand and let the largest rock know him, laying his palm on it's surface until his heat began to warm it's surface. He whispered "I am Frost of Home. I seek a ride to the high ridge." When the rocks began to dive and leap again, he knew that they were ready for him.

He climbed carefully onto the back of the largest boulder. It was a pale grey, almost blue. The boulder eased forward, splitting the turf at its base, sinking into the ground until Frost's feet began to nudge the small white flowers that grew there. The wet smell of broken earth filled his nose, and there was a sound like fabric being slowly torn as the boulder moved through the soft dirt. It moved faster and faster to the peak of the hill and then leapt.

Frost let his hands loose, extending them wide as he rode the boulder through the air to the next shifting hill. Smaller rocks were flying with them, and the school sliced into the next hill as easily as birds dove through the clouds. Frost laughed and grabbed the boulder again as it swam to the next peak and leapt again.

From one shifting sea of earth and grass to the next, climbing the ever-changing landscape in the only way that would not leave one lost and directionless, Frost was carried to the mountain ridge beyond the hills. The sun reached its zenith as brown earth gave way to blood-red rock. The boulder slowed and Frost knew that the time had come for him to climb off. He knelt next to the boulder and placed his forehead against it, thanking the rock for sharing its joy with him, and providing him with a safe journey to the ridge. When he rose to his feet, the school of rocks had submerged beneath the scraggly remnants of green grass and he knew they would ride the waves of earth all the way back down to the fields below.

He saw one small rock dive out of the ground and twist in the sunlight, flashing its reflections at him.

The ridge that led up Sleeping Mountain was no playful space, and Frost walked carefully. Whereas the hills below the mountain rolled and slid like young animals playing while schools of rocks swum and danced through them, the ridgeline jutted and jagged. Deep movements below the dark, sharp surface would erupt in sudden fingers of stone that tore into the world the mountain shared with Frost and his people. He stepped slowly, and moved around outcrops that leaned over him angrily.

Frost pricked his ears, listening for the sound of Sleeping Mountain. His grandmother had told him to listen for the voice of the mountain as he walked, but now he was afraid that he would not be able to hear it. Wind filled his ears, a keening whine that rose and fell but never became silent. The sound of gravel crunching beneath his feet seemed like the crash of a storm. He winced as the edges of the rocks dug into the soles of his feet. Tough as they were, he had not experienced a path as cruel as this ridgeline.

Grandmother Sky had also told him to watch for the Song, and so he looked for the small blue butterflies as he walked. There were far fewer of them so high, far from the grass and flowers below. However, some sat sunning themselves on rocks, their wings lifting and opening to the light. Suddenly, a cluster of the Song nearest Frost flapped into the air and began to fly away from him.

A new sound sought his attention. Frost felt it through his heels first, a silent pressure that built against his feet. He felt as though he was about to be flung into the air. Then the sound grew, as though it was coming from far behind him, approaching him faster and faster, louder and louder. Frost threw himself forward, crying out as a rock struck his knee and split his skin.

Behind him the path burst and a long thin spear of stone launched up. Rocks and pebbles clattered to the ground around him, but Frost covered his face with an arm and waited until the voice of the mountain subsided. He touched the cut on his leg with one hand. Though it was bleeding and tender, he could see that the wound was not serious. He pushed himself to his feet and shifted his weight back and forth to test the leg. It held.

Some of the Song began to flutter back down to the rocky surface of the ridge, laying on the smooth rock, sunning themselves once more. Frost understood why Tide had sung them and made the mountain sleep. He was terrified of what the mountain may have done if it were awake.

Frost followed the ridgeline, the one landmark that stayed still, until the zigzag backbone of Sleeping Mountain reached its end. The sun was now following its set path down towards the horizon. He would have to move quickly if he was to return home with enough Waddling Redbeaks for dinner. He stood at the crest of the ridge, looking down a steep slope into the valley between the peaks. New outcrops of dark stone burst around the lip of the bowl while he watched, grinding with terrifying strength into the air, and then the ground opened alongside him.

Long thin holes tore the ground on either side of the path Frost stood upon. Geysers of steam blasted into the air, whistling and shrieking with released pressure. Frost crouched down and was glad that the openings were not close enough for him to be harmed. He waited as the steam waned and then blew away on the wind, then stood and placed the flatcakes he had brought from his father on the rocks. He laid a hand on the rock as he spoke.

"Thank you for protecting this place and allowing me to enter it." He left his hand in place as the ground shifted once more. The torn ground lifted and resettled until it was hard to see where the openings had been. Then Frost stood and bowed to the mountain.

Frost began the careful climb down into the valley. Scree shifted beneath his feet and hands, and he slid more than he climbed. Getting back out would be difficult. Frost looked back and up the slope that lay behind him, then swung his head away and sheltered himself with his arms as a new outcrop pushed forward high above, showering him once more with gravel and small stones. Further down, the slope levelled out into a grassy bowl, broad and calm, sheltered from the wind. Far overhead the sun beamed down on Frost. A blue and black butterfly, part of Tide's song, fluttered past on its journey between the flowers that speckled the field here. Frost stood on the grass and dusted himself off, then admired the slope. Stones still trickled and tumbled down from the heights.

Frost could see, at the end of the fields, a cluster of low bushes that grew close beneath a waterfall that trickled from another ridge above. The walk to the bushes took a long time. The earth beneath the grass was soft, and his feet sank deep with every step. The sun warmed the back of his neck, and Frost felt sweat begin to chafe his body as he walked.

When he arrived at the bushes, he could see that the thin waterfall dropped into a placid pool of water between the thick bushes. From the small pool, a tiny stream wound away to his left, seeking a pathway out of the sheltered valley, before it drained away into a cave in the rocks so small that Frost had to walk much closer before he was sure that a cave was there. Frost heard the voice of his Grandmother Sky, and so he knelt next to the small pool and cupped his hands in the water. He lifted the clear water to his mouth and drank and smiled. It was truly pure enough to clean the clouds.

Somewhere in these bushes, the Redbeaks that his mother wanted must be hiding. Frost pulled the snare from his carry bag. The snare was woven from rushes during long evenings in his parent's home, as they shared stories of the past. He set it up at the base of a bush and then moved away to hide. The bushes were made of very thin branches that stabbed in multiple directions, and grew thick stubby dark-green leaves. Hiding deep within the bushes, hidden in the crook of some branches, were small pairs of round red fruits. Frost admired the way the fruits shone and reflected the sunlight.

He didn't have to wait long before a loud squawk broke the peaceful still of the valley. Frost returned to find a Redbeak bound and scrambling in the dirt. He held out his hand towards the animal and then thanked it for the meal he would make of it. Then he broke its neck. He looked at the bird that lay on the ground before him. It had a fat belly, and long spindly legs. He considered how many of his family's friends had been invited to dinner. Frost unwound the rush snare from the Redbeak's legs and then set it again.

After catching and killing a second Redbeak, Frost took another flatcake out of his carry bag and broke it into crumbs. He scattered the crumbs under the bush where he had set his snare. As he threw the small pieces of cake to the ground, he spoke his thanks to the Redbeaks and the valley. Frost spoke lowly, only just loud enough for his own ears to hear him. Then he bowed to the bushes, and began his journey back across the fields, between the butterflies. The climb back up the sliding stones to the high ridge was more difficult now, burdened as he was by the bodies of the two fat birds slung over his shoulders. However, he gritted his teeth and concentrated, and soon he was standing where Sleeping Mountain continued to breach and stretch.

Once upon the spine of Sleeping Mountain, Frost moved carefully but quickly back along the ridge until he found a safe passage down to the rolling hills. Now his journey was much easier than it had been on the way up. He walked with the waves, and so was carried gently from peak to peak and back to the edge of Swarming Forest. The trees reached out for him like old friends who had missed him, curious about the birds that he carried. He tapped the spindly twigs and they retreated, leaving him to walk along the shadowy forest path unbothered. He waved at the keepers he passed on his way through the forest and back to Home.

III. "TO THE GATHERING"

When Frost walked back between the buildings of Home, something was wrong. No children played between the houses, and few people were cooking or cleaning or weaving outside their homes. Frost took the birds to his family's house and hung them from a hook just inside the doorway, before turning to look for a sign of what was going on.

A young man whose name meant the sound of waves rolling up the sand was jogging by. Frost called out to him.

"Where is everyone Sand?"

"At the beach. Some strange thing has flown to us."

Frost wondered what Sand meant, but had no time to ask before his friend jogged out of sight along the path that led out of Home. Frost decided to follow. He walked out of the village and along the winding pass between tall singular trees, until he came to the long grass that marked the beginning of the dunes above the broad beach. He climbed up through the dunes and when he reached the top he was shocked by what he saw.

A large thing was floating above the pale sand, grey and red and curved, exactly like a gigantic rock. But thick shining straps wrapped around the thing and hung down from it to a long building with many windows underneath. A ladder dangled from the building and there were people crowding around the bottom of the ladder. Most of them were Frost's fellow villagers, but a knot in the middle were strangers. Their clothes were made of strange materials, and coloured blue and yellow as brightly as birds. Frost began to run down the hill to find out who they were.

"What is all this?" he asked his mother as he ran up next to her in the crowd.

"No one knows," Calling-Bird replied, reaching out an arm to slip it around his shoulder and pull him close. She leaned over his head and kissed it. "Be careful for now."

Frost's sister Ray was next to their mother, clutching an arm around Calling-Bird's legs. She looked over at her brother.

"I don't like this," she said.

"I'm sure they mean no harm," he replied. "Everything will be okay. There are so many Villagers here, you will be safe."

"That's not what I mean," she grouched, and she turned back to watch what was going on.

Frost watched as one of the strangers began to walk forward slowly. He had a long rectangular beard, and his clothing hung down behind him like a beetle's shell, bright yellow. His hands were held up at the height of his shoulders, palms facing towards the villagers.

The village leader, whose name meant the warmth of coals through the night, stepped forward as well, holding her own arms up in the same gesture. Coal called out to the stranger "What is your name? What lands have you come from? Can we offer you anything?"

Frost was surprised when the man answered in the

language of the Villagers. Frost had been sure that the man would sound different to them, as different as the Twintail's morning song was different to the bark of a dog.

"I am pleased to be a visitor to this land. My name is Gulrick." Frost mouthed the harsh sound that the stranger claimed was his name. Frost wondered what the sound meant.

"My lands are many months away, in my skyboat." The stranger pointed at the huge thing that floated above them. Looking at it from this closer vantage, Frost saw the skyboat bobbing in the breeze, and realised that it was anchored to the ground by a long rope.

"They are lands of tall grey mountains, and snow. You would not know their names, but they are-" Frost could not understand the sounds that followed. It sounded as though the stranger was coughing and growling, all at once.

"We ask to share in your food and your water, and will gladly offer what we can share in return," finished the stranger. He stepped cautiously forward and met one of Coal's upheld hands with his own, pressing the palm to hers. Then he stepped back three paces and bowed deeply.

"How does he know the correct way to meet new people?" Frost looked up at his mother's face. She was not smiling, but she did not seem worried.

"I don't know," she answered without looking back at him. "He may be a stranger from very far away, and he may look very unusual to our eyes, but perhaps manners are the same everywhere?"

Then Frost saw someone who looked just like his own uncle, whose name meant the faint lines of high cloud on a bright summer's day, standing with the strangers near their ladder. He was about to run forward and greet Cloud, but then he realised that it was not the same man. His uncle Cloud wore a sharp tattoo on his upper arms that showed his skill with net-making and fishing, but this man had none.

"Who is the man with them?" asked Frost.

"I do not know," laughed his mother, who tousled his hair. "You know the same things that I do today!"

The man with the rectangular beard glanced over his shoulder at the familiar stranger. There was a small nod from the figure. Frost wondered who the second man was, and how he could have some control over the rectangle bearded man who had spoken to Coal.

Coal was still speaking to the new people, but they looked at her with blank faces that did not move. She frowned and tried to speak again. This time the man who looked like Frost's uncle Cloud stepped forward, head lowered and hands to his sides, speaking softly. The man with the rectangle beard glanced at the untattooed man and then looked at Coal. The man with the rectangle beard spoke slowly and there was a strange tone to his words. Frost realised that the man did not understand what the words he was saying meant.

"Plenty to you and your people," he began. "I am from a land far away, and come to share stories with the people of this land. I do not wish there to be anger between us, and offer this gift as a sign of friendship."

The untattooed man now held out a small box. The man with the rectangle beard took the box and passed it to Coal who looked into it. Her eyes widened and her mouth fell open, then she looked back up with a strong smile. She gestured for the villagers to come forward also.

Frost's people moved forward with smiles to investigate the newcomers closer. The visitors responded with a strange expression, pulling their lips wide and squinting at the villagers. Frost felt nervous when he saw them make this face, but the untattooed man spoke loudly to the villagers, explaining that the visitors' expression was how they showed happiness. He introduced himself now, saying that his name was the sense of justice that thrives in generous hearts and that he came from an island named Safety, far across the ocean. Frost moved forward with his neighbours, letting go of his mother's hand. Ray stayed close by Calling-Bird, gripping her mother's hand tight.

Ray called after Frost as he ran forward, but he did not hear. He rushed along with the other youths. The visitor nearest to him was a tall man with a very short beard of tight curls. His eyes were dark and his face was stretched in the same expression as the other visitors. Frost saw that he was holding a long staff, with carvings down the sides that were golden like the sun. The way the jagged shape shone enticed Frost, and he reached out towards the staff.

"Eeegyaoh!" yelped the man, and he jerked away, swinging the staff as he did and knocking Frost's hands aside.

Frost was stunned. He clutched at his wrist. Around him he heard shouting and was knocked to the ground by bodies shoving their way past him. When Frost blinked and looked up, it was into the angry faces of his neighbours and relatives.

"Please not things!" The voice was stilted and confused. "Not thing of purpose!"

Everyone looked around, including the red faced visitors who were pointing their staffs at Frost's angry peers. The man with the rectangle beard had both his hands high in the air and Justice was standing next to him, whispering into his ear, trying to suggest words.

"This thing was not real." The man shook his head. "Mistake. Go back, go back!" This instruction was given to the visitors. Slowly, and carefully, they began to lower the staffs and step away from the villagers. Frost's neighbours looked down at him and then stepped away as well.

A hand reached down to Frost. It was the man whose staff he had tried to touch. The eyes watching him at the other end of that arm were unsure. Frost reached out and let the man pull him to his feet. He could feel the weight of the people surrounding him lift as he stood and nodded at the man. Frost rubbed his wrist again but then rolled his hand around at the end of his arm. It ached a bit from being hit, but he would be fine.

The man made the strange stretched expression again, and then held out his staff to Frost. This time when he touched it, the visitor did not get startled. The man with the rectangle beard laughed and called out loudly. Frost did not understand what the man was saying, but it seemed as though everyone was happy now.

The visitors were led back over the dunes and into Home by the crowd of villagers. As tradition dictated, the visitors were welcomed into different homes and spent the evening having meals with many families. They brought gifts of food from their skyboat, many strange things that the villagers had never tasted before. Some of them were savoury and made Frost's mouth dry, while others were sweeter than the honey that the villagers gathered in their hives.

Three of the visitors came to share a meal with Frost and his family. They stopped outside the door to Frost's home and laid their hands on the walls. When his grandmother called them inside they responded by saying their names and origins, and asking to share a meal with the family. Frost could tell that they did not understand what they were saying, just like the man with the rectangular beard had not known what his speech meant. Neither could Frost understand the names of the people or their places.

After reciting their introduction, the visitors entered. They sat cross legged around the low table that Calling-Bird had set up in the middle of the home, all sitting nearest the door. Frost was surprised to see that they knew the correct place for guests. Whoever had taught them how to introduce themselves and behave had done a good job. One of the visitors shuffled awkwardly on the cushion that Frost's mother had provided.

On the other side of the table, Frost could see Ray sitting with narrowed eyes. She tapped her fingers on her knee and watched the visitors carefully, studying every move they made. Where Frost was impressed at their manners, Ray seemed to snort and grow more annoyed by their every action.

The visitors brought large white bowls full of crunchy green vegetables to share, and some bottles of a drink that Frost's parents would not let him try. They knew very little of the villagers' language, but it seemed that they had been taught the correct words to say, acknowledging the generosity of the home allowing them to mingle with the family inside.

Grandmother Sky came in quietly and sat to the side of the room, watching everyone. As guests, the visitors were encouraged to take the first pieces of food from the platters on the low table. Frost waited until he could see a small nod from his grandmother, when she was satisfied that the guests were enjoying their first taste of the meal, before he reached out himself.

Without much shared language, the villagers and the visitors mostly spoke among their separate groups, but Frost was curious about these strange new people. He tried to find out what words they did understand, and used mime to help him learn more.

Everyone tried to share their names with one another again, though the visitors had trouble repeating Frost's family's names in full. They kept stopping halfway and then nodding as though they had mastered the names, a sight that made Frost giggle. He himself found their names difficult as well, not because they were long, but because they were so short. The man who had shifted on his cushion seemed to be known as Luter, but Frost wondered what the sounds meant. The tall woman was Berith, and the man with long dark hair and small eyes was called Zelig.

With difficulty, the three visitors explained that they had come to learn about the land, because it was so far from their own homes. Frost wasn't sure, but it seemed as though they each had different things that they wanted to find out about. He made clear that he would love to help them learn all they could. They made their strange face-stretching expression and his own parents laughed and patted him on the back.

IV. "WHERE WE ALL SHARE"

Frost's first chance to help the visitors came the very next morning. All three of the visitors came back to his home and waited outside until Grandmother Sky came to the door and welcomed them inside. Frost smiled. It was strange that they would wait like this again, but at least it showed that they were trying to be well mannered. Once the three were inside they used their limited words and lots of wide hand gestures to communicate that they would like to be shown around the land by Frost.

He jumped up and raced over to Sky who nodded, and then he gathered some food into his carry bag and beckoned the visitors to come with him. Before they could leave, Ray stepped forward as well.

"I would like to come with you," she announced. "I need the exercise after being stuck at home for so long."

"Certainly," agreed Frost.

Together the group headed beyond the village and Frost

led the way to Swarming Forest. As they walked, Frost tried to learn as much of the visitors' language as he could, and shared his own words for the things they saw as they walked.

They entered Swarming Forest along the narrow dusty path. Frost paused and ducked to avoid branches swinging by his head. He pulled on the visitors' clothes to stop them wandering off the path, and he felt his stomach drop as he considered what would happen if they were to step on land without the tree's approval. He had seen animals skewered by the trees, but never people.

The man who had shifted on his cushion reached out towards a flowering vine that dangled near them.

"Stop," said Ray before the visitor could touch the flower. "What are you doing?"

"I collect plants," said the shifting man. "I would like to collect this and take it to my home. To learn more about it."

Ray turned to meet Frost's eyes. He could see confusion in them, creasing their corners. He knew what she must be thinking. How could someone learn more about a living thing like a tree by taking it away from where it lived? Would it not become a different thing once it was removed from the world it belonged to?

"But the trees may not like that," she said.

The shifting man blinked and looked around. Frost could tell that he had not considered what the trees would think.

"I would keep only a little piece," he said slowly. He reached out again.

Neither Ray or Frost moved to stop the man. Frost watched uncomfortably, flinching as the man's fingers tightened around a thin leafy vine. Keepers watched from high above in the canopy, though Frost did not think the visitors had noticed them. They did not seem to be rushing down to stop the shifting man, but Frost still thought it was not a good decision.

The man pulled at the flowering vine and cut it loose with a knife and then carefully bundled the vine and it's flowers into a bag that hung from his hip.

Frost shifted his weight back and forth on his feet. He saw the keepers riding high in the canopy, keeping a close eye on what was happening on the path. He could tell that they were not angry, but concerned. Frost wondered how Swarming Forest would react to the shifting man now.

Beside him, Ray reached out a hand to a nearby trunk and laid it on the rough wood. She closed her eyes and Frost watched her lips move as she said something to the trees. Then she removed her hand and bowed.

On the path behind them the long-haired visitor had stopped still for a long time, holding a small shining object out in his hand, leaning close over it. Frost approached the man in order to get away from the cut vine that hung slack overhead.

"What is that?" asked Frost.

"It is a direction-holder," replied the visitor, using half-words and gesture to get the meaning across. He pulled out an object like a block of wood, slightly longer than his hand and four fingers deep. The block split and revealed pale leaves that opened like the petals of a flower. The long-haired man began drawing a picture on the leaves with a black stick.

"What are you doing?"

"This is a Map." The short sound was strange to Frost, and he looked closely at the drawing. He wanted to understand what a Map was. "I am making a picture of what the land looks like."

Frost watched, fascinated by the pictures that the visitor was making. They did not look like the land that he knew, they were strange uneven ovals instead of tall jagged lines like the trees he could see.

Ray came over to look at the Map as well. She peered over

Frost's shoulder and shook her head. "But this part of the land doesn't look like that?"

"It would if you were up there." The long-haired man pointed into a patch of sky visible far above the tops of Swarming Forest. The small shadow of a bird passed between them and the clouds. "This is what everything looks like from our skyboat."

Frost tried to imagine what the land would look like if he was leaning out of the strange flying building that the visitors had arrived in. It was difficult, but he had looked out at the land while he walked the ridge of Sleeping Mountain, and so he had some idea of what the land looked from such a lofty position. He thought that the forest would still look like spikes, but knew better than to argue with someone when he had no experience of the situation.

"Come, I would like to show you more," Frost told the three visitors.

He led them through Swarming Forest to the edge of the hills beyond, the place where boulders swim. They were rolling and turning across each other, like puppies playing in their house. Frost smiled and watched as a small school of stone flashed at the top of one hill.

The three visitors stood and stared, with mouths wide open. The long-haired man slowly pulled out his leaf block and began sketching in it, but then shook his head.

Frost heard the visitor muttering, but could not understand the words that the man used, so he asked the man to explain.

"I was to say that this is hard." The long-haired man pointed at the hills with his drawing stick. "They move and the picture does not." He held out the Map to Frost again.

Frost frowned as he looked at the strange drawing. Now

that he was standing outside Swarming Forest, he felt as though he was beginning to understand the way it worked. He could see the slowly curving edge of the forest as it stretched away to either side of the last ebbing foothills, stretching forward and drawing back. And here on the drawing was a line that seemed to be the same as that one.

"Could you just mark where they are as a family, but not each hill itself?" asked Frost.

The man took back the Map and looked at it for a moment. Eventually he nodded.

"It will do. I can make more correct later time." He added lines to his map.

The small group sat on the grass below the hills and shared their food. Ray ate silently, watching the visitors, while Frost tried to talk with them. It was difficult, but new words became clear with every sentence. The long-haired man showed him other leaves in his block, explaining that they were Maps of other places the visitors had seen. Frost stared at the round shapes and wished he understood. The leaves were also covered with black insect trails that the man said spoke to him. Frost did not understand.

Once they had finished their food, Frost stood and pointed to where a school of rocks were circling low on a small hillside.

"Shall we play with them?" he asked.

"It is enough to see today," said the man with the long hair. "We do not know swimming rocks, and may be dangerous." Frost thought of how he rode the rocks higher and higher through the hills, flying through the air on their backs, reaching the heights of the ridge along the back of Sleeping Mountain. His father had spoken to him of needing caution on the ridgeline, but trusted him amongst the hills. That had been but a day earlier.

However, he couldn't judge how safe these visitors would feel in the dancing hills, and so he did not argue. He was sure they would let him know if they wanted him to show them more another time.

Together the group made their way back into Swarming Forest, walking slowly along the paths as it's trunks and boughs swung ponderously past. Frost did not need to pull the visitors back onto the path this time, and the keepers watched only from afar.

By the time they returned to the house in the village, the three visitors looked tired. Frost felt as though his day had just begun and so he left them to rest in his home and then went fishing with some other young people from Home. He asked Ray to come, but she told him that she wanted to stay in their home, to prepare dinner with Calling-Bird and Grandmother Sky. Frost was sure that she wanted to keep watching the visitors.

While he lay back in the narrow boat with two other youths, rocking in the ocean swells and listening to the hollow clonk of the boat rising and falling, they asked him what the visitors were like. He explained how they were curious about everything they saw in the world, and how they spent much of their time drawing pictures of what they had found.

When he returned home with his catch, he moved around to the back of the house, where there was a space for cleaning and filleting the fish so that it could be cooked for dinner. As he scrubbed the scales off the fish, Frost smiled as he thought about his day with the visitors.

Frost placed a hand on the side of the fish and bowed his head, sitting motionless in the dying light, then lifted his knife and set to his task. The remains that would not feed his family, he buried beneath some of the plants in the garden near his home. He stood and bowed before brushing the dirt off his hands. Then he scooped some water out of the rain barrel to finish washing them properly before going inside.

"Are the visitors still here?" he asked Ray.

"No. They returned to the beach and their skyboat."

Frost felt disappointed. He wanted to learn more from them.

V. "A SONG KNOWN"

No visitors came the next day. Frost did not know what to do with himself. He wandered through the nearby fields and spoke with his neighbours about the crops. He visited some Villagers in their homes, and asked about their families. Everyone was well. In the afternoon he walked through the long thin grass on the dunes and stood looking down at the beach. The skyboat hovered above the sand like a bird in an updraft, motionless in the wind. Waves crashed beyond the grey building.

When the visitors returned the following morning, Frost jumped up from the ground outside his home and ran to meet them.

"Will we see more today?" he asked excitedly.

The long-haired man laughed and nodded. "We would like you to take us back."

Before Frost could agree, Ray came running out of the doorway.

"I'm coming with you," she declared.

This time Frost was not as pleased with his sister.

"Why do you want to come?" he asked in a hushed voice. "You do not enjoy spending time with the visitors."

"They may be dangerous. You need someone with you."

"They are not dangerous!" he insisted. But there was no way to dissuade her, and she came with them as they walked.

The visitors did not stop during the passage through Swarming Forest. When Frost tried to show them some of the strange trees that did not visit the path often, the visitors only seemed to frown. Could they not tell that the ancient trees were curious to see these newcomers? Frost felt as though he had done something wrong, but he sighed and led them to the hills where the boulders swam.

Here he received the response that he longed for from the three visitors. They paused again, staring at the hills and the schools of rock that could be seen. He laughed at their expressions, delighted that he could show them such things that they had not seen before.

"Will you dance with them?" he asked, hoping that now he could take them riding upon the boulders.

The long-haired man shook his head again. "Not yet. But we look closer." He took out his shiny object again, turning and looking along the side of Swarming Forest.

"The trees do not come here?" he asked, pointing to the edge of the forest.

"Why would they?" asked Frost.

"They move. But not move here?"

Again, Frost was confused. Why would the trees leave the safety and security of their families?

"They do not need to," he said.

A brilliant blue Song flew by. Its broad wings fluttered and it lighted upon one of the broad white flowers near Frost and the visitors. The tall woman stepped forward slowly, reaching out with slightly hooked fingers. The butterfly sunned itself, raising and lowering its wings with the patience of a mother. Then the visitor lunged, flicking her hand forward with a speed that surprised Frost. She trapped the butterfly within a cage made of her long fingers. She turned, and her mouth was pulled open into the visitor's strange expression.

"Success," she said loudly, and she bounced on her feet in excitement.

"Why have you captured that butterfly?" asked Ray.

"To look at it closely," answered the tall woman. She frowned and held her hand up. "It is new."

"New?" Ray looked confused. "It is one of Tide's Songs. There are many of them." She turned to point across the shifting hills, where dozens of blue butterflies could be seen. "What makes the Song you are holding so special to you?"

"It is new for us." she explained, using her free hand to mime some of the meaning for Frost and his sister. Carefully the tall woman lowered her pack to the ground and then pulled out her own leaf block like the one the shifting man had. She also pulled out a small cage made of thin sticks that she transferred the butterfly into. Then she sat down on a large rock and began making drawings and marks on the leaves of her block. Frost watched her, wondering what the marks she made would say to her. The other visitors took the chance to eat some food that they had brought in their own packs.

After a while the rock she was sitting on sank into the ground. Frost knew it had woken up and wished to join the other rocks as they leapt from hilltop to hilltop. The woman did not know this, and she yelped in panic and then laughed.

"Do the rocks all do this?" she asked Frost from where she lay on the grass.

"They enjoy swimming the hills," he replied with a shrug.

He convinced them to follow him closer to the hills, and was rewarded by some small rocks that looped towards them. The three adults moved closer together, and eyed the rocks circling them as though the grey and brown stones were dangerous animals. Frost tried to convince the visitors to hold out their hands to meet the rocks, but they refused as one. Eventually he led them all back through Swarming Forest to Home.

As they came close to Frost's home, he asked if they would stay for dinner with his family again. The long-haired man spoke quietly with his companions and then agreed. Frost led them inside, but then his friend, whose name meant the brightness of the evening star, came to the door and asked if Frost wanted to swim in the sea. Frost was torn. He looked around his home at the visitors and his family. Ray had settled herself next to Calling-Bird and watched him back. But his mother shooed him out the door.

"We will take care of these visitors. You go enjoy yourself."

At the beach, Frost and Star jumped in the waves and lay down on their stomachs to glide along with the churning water as it rolled into the beach. They swam out past the white tips and lay back on the ocean, watching the clouds that floated through the blue sky overhead.

"You have spent a lot of time with these new people," said Star.

Frost did not reply.

"What are they like?"

"They are fascinating. They want to learn all they can about the land here. They have so many strange things."

He described the direction-holder and the Map. Star thought these things were strange, but was not as interested in them as Frost was. Her eyes grew wide as Frost described the way one visitor had snatched a butterfly out of the air without so much as bruising the small creature's wings.

"They are fantastic, are they not!" she declared.

Frost agreed.

The water began to feel cold, so Frost and Star swam back to the beach and walked back into the village. Star continued to ask about the visitors and Frost shared as much as he could. Finally they shared a quick hug and Frost walked inside his home.

Here he found the long-haired man was slowly and carefully copying drawings of the forest and hills into a larger block of leaves. There were less of the small marks on the new drawings, and Frost asked why.

"I made marks about the land when we were there," said the visitor, though Frost wasn't really sure what he meant. "Now I put them on a new Map. I don't need the marks now."

Frost smiled but was confused. He moved on to the next visitor.

The shifting man had laid the stick that he had plucked from the forest into a small wooden box. Now he made many marks on his leaf block.

"Why do you have more marks than he did?" asked Frost, pointing at the long-haired man.

"Because the plant goes with the marks," said the shifting man. "I say where the plant was. I tell how the tree was too."

"Why did you only keep part of the tree at all if you wanted to know all of it?" asked Ray from the far side of the room.

"How else would I know a thing? If I don't have vine, what I say to other people at home?"

"You could tell them about the Keepers, and how we must stick to the paths," began Ray. She frowned and looked at Frost. "Studying a tree by keeping one twig is like trying to understand the sea by examining the ripples in a rock pool."

The visitor frowned and Frost wondered if he understood what she had said.

The tall woman was hunched over her work and Frost had to move in close if he wanted to see what she was doing. He gasped.

The visitor had a small wooden frame set on her lap, and she had angled it to catch as much light from the windows as she could. It was square, like a box, but very shallow. At the back of the frame was a smooth pale wooden surface, and set on that surface was the butterfly that the visitor had caught and kept in her small wicker cage.

Frost could see a shining stick, thinner than a splinter, sticking out of the motionless Song. His sister hissed quietly from behind him. He hadn't heard her walk up.

"What have you done?" she asked.

"I pinned this butterfly in a box, to carry it home." The visitor turned and lifted the box to show Frost and his sister. The tall woman's face split into the strange expression that the visitors displayed so often, revealing her white teeth.

"Is it asleep?" Ray asked.

"No, it is dead," answered the tall woman.

Ray lifted a hand to her mouth.

"Why did you need to kill it?"

The visitor blinked. "It could not live in skyboat until we get home. Too far!"

"Then maybe you could have left it here."

"Shush Ray," said Frost, placing a hand on his sister's shoulder. "They are finding out so much about the world! It's important work!"

Ray glared at Frost and then left.

"Can I have a closer look?" he asked the visitor. She nodded and handed the frame over to him.

"Be careful. I be sad if box hurt. Very precious!"

Frost nodded and leaned in closer. It was incredible to see the thin lines that criss crossed the bright blue of the creature's wings so closely. He saw the wispy antenna tremble as he breathed nearby. Then he returned the frame to the visitor.

"Thank you so much," he said.

"Thank you for showing me," answered the tall woman.

VI. "FOR HARMONY"

Two days later the long-haired man returned and asked for Frost.

"I don't know why you keep spending time with them," hissed his sister as he walked past her.

"Why wouldn't I spend time with them? They are learning so much about the land and they share what they know with me."

"There's something wrong with them."

"How can you say that? They have tried to treat us with good manners. They have shared their knowledge with us. They have done no harm." He paused and looked into her eyes. "I think you might be jealous."

"What!?" she squawked. Before she could gather herself, Frost left and began walking with the long-haired man toward Swarming Forest.

"It is just you?" he asked the man, who he remembered was called Zelig.

"Yes."

"Why?"

Zelig stretched his face when he looked at Frost.

"Busy, work."

Frost nodded. They must have so much to do to understand what they had found. He looked through the trees in the forest as they followed the path and frowned. Something seemed different in the dark space beneath the canopy. He paused and looked harder. Zelig stopped a few metres along the path and looked back at him, waiting.

Frost looked out through the trunks and tried to figure out what had caught his eye. Everything seemed just as it should be. Shadows shifted and dappled sun spots flowed over the undergrowth. Was it moving slower than it should, he wondered. He looked up at the canopy overhead, the highest and oldest trees stretching themselves out to shield the others from something overhead. Those high distant boughs barely seemed to quiver.

"Okay?" asked Zelig from his spot a little further along the path.

"Yes," Frost answered slowly. There was nothing he could be sure of, and so he squared his shoulders and resumed the walk with the older man.

When they reached the place where boulders swim, Zelig was excited to try riding the stones for the first time. Frost led him to a quiet spot at the bottom of the hills and waited for a school of rocks to notice them and come closer. He had to keep placing a hand on Zelig's elbow, as the man would try to start walking up the hills without already meeting the rocks. Frost tried to explain that the rocks would need to come to him first, but Zelig did not seem to understand.

As they waited, Frost looked around the fields. Something seemed unusual here as well. Stones flashed their reflection of the sun's light as they swum through the hills behind him, but the fields between the hills and the forest seemed quieter than usual. They were always peaceful and calm, but this seemed the stillness of a garden that had been plucked clean, not the comfortable stillness of a home sheltering a sleeping family.

Before Frost could identify what made him feel uneasy, there was a ripping sound from behind him. He turned to see a small group of rocks easing their way through the grass towards himself and Zelig. He guided Zelig forward, lifting a hand and waiting for the rock to move forward and touch them. Zelig tried to move his hand away and climb onto the rock, but again Frost had to calm the man's excitement.

"The rocks do not know you yet," he said. "You must explain who you are, and what you need."

Zelig muttered in his spiky language, and Frost did not understand what the man said. He hoped that the rock would understand. They waited with their hands on the rough surface of the stones. Frost felt his rock shift as it knew him, and he could tell that the boulders were now comfortable with his presence. He stood to walk around them but saw that the visitor was still waiting.

"We can move now," he said.

"What? But why?" grunted Zelig, tossing his head to shift his hair from his face.

Frost tried to explain, but it was too hard when they knew so few of each other's words.

These rocks were large and old, curious but gentle. They rode up and over the crest of the hills, then down the far slopes before climbing the next again. Frost lay forward and enjoyed the air rushing over his cheeks and blowing in his eyes, grinning and laughing as his rock swum through the land. The ride was exhilarating, but there were less stones leaping from hill to hill today. Even the sun seemed cooler. Behind him he saw

Zelig gripping tightly to his stone with every finger hooked into a crevice, knees and feets anchored deeply. The man looked frightened.

When they reached the ridge of the mountain, Frost paused.

"It is dangerous here," he said. He looked along the ridgeline as long jagged spires pushed inexorably up, like the spines on a sea urchin.

"You show me safe?" asked Zelig.

Frost swallowed. He wondered if he really would be able to keep the man safe here. He felt very young now, standing in these high places, with someone who did not seem to understand what it meant to be here. He patted his carry bag.

"I will."

They began to walk along the ridgeline.

Frost could feel the heart of the mountain beneath his feet. It shivered and grumbled. The mountain was uneasy. However there were still a few blue butterflies resting on the rocks all around them, sunning their wings slowly. He stepped around large blocks that stood in the way, and guided Zelig in loops that avoided open spaces. He could see that the visitor wondered why they moved in such ways, so he began to point at the spikes of stone that burst through the path they could have taken. Soon Zelig was taking care to stay behind Frost, and to place his feet exactly in Frost's footprints.

"How far?" asked Frost. He could see that the grove he had travelled to only a few days earlier was not far ahead. He wondered where he might need to place his thanks to the mountain. He heard the mountain shift again and wondered whether it would accept his offer of thanks.

"Need to see," was Zelig's reply. The man seemed to stretch up as high as he could, shielding his eyes from the sun and looking around. Then he would drop back onto the flat of his feet and shrug. "No see far from this place."

Frost showed Zelig the way to a tall mound, just to the side of the path. He helped the man climb up the loose gravel sides and then scrabbled up alongside him. Together they stood on the mound and surveyed the lands around the mountain.

When he looked back the way they had come, Frost could see the place where the boulders swim, the forest and beyond that he could just make out the dark smudge that was his village. All the buildings that he knew, and all the people he loved, all were contained in that small smear against the green land. Beyond the village spread a blue sparkling sea.

But then he turned around and beheld more of the land.

Mountains spread into the distance to his left, some even taller and sharper than the mountain he stood on. He wondered how far they stretched and whether anyone lived amongst those white heights. Valleys cut through the foothills in that direction. A river flowed away from him in another direction, beyond the valley where he had caught the wading birds. It was broad and brown, and forests clustered near it's edge like animals drinking their fill in the wide flat green space.

Zelig crouched down and pulled out his leaf block. He opened it and began to make marks, rushed and scratchy marks as he drew with haste. He looked as though he thought that the world would vanish before him at any moment, perhaps covered by a cloth and hidden from his sight. Frost looked over his shoulder.

"How does the Map work?" he asked.

Zelig paused and looked up at the young man. Then he reached up and put an arm across Frost's shoulder, pulling him down to look at the pictures he had made. He began to point at the shapes on his leaf, circles and triangles, insect trails that spoke.

"Here, this is mountain. And here, this is mountain." As he spoke, he pointed from the shapes on his leaf to the mountains they could see. One was the mountain beneath their feet, another was the tallest of the white spears far far away. "This is gaps." He shook his head. "Bad mountains." He frowned again.

"Valleys?" suggested Frost. He pointed at one of the valleys and said the word again.

Zelig nodded. "Valleys."

He showed Frost how he drew the forests and the rivers into his map. He stabbed at the leaf with his drawing stick.

"I can stick the places I have seen on here. Pin them down. Then I can study them." He poked into the leaf with his drawing stick once more. "I can take these places home with me."

Frost looked at the shapes on the leaf. He wondered how the man would take these lands home.

"These will tell me about the land." Zelig pointed at the insect marks he had made next to the shapes. Again, Frost wondered how these scratchy black marks could speak to the visitors. Would they tell the stories of the land to the visitors when they returned to their home? How did these marks know of Tide and the way he sang the mountain to sleep? Frost looked out at the white spears near the horizon. He didn't know what stories those mountains held. Did the marks on the leaf know them?

There was a thundering roar, and the mountain swatted at the annoyances who had climbed upon their back. Thick stumps of rock lifted from the surface of the ridge, moving the mound and rolling Frost and Zelig from it. Frost leapt as the ground turned, managing to land and roll along sharp stones, using his arms to protect his head. He turned to see if the visitor was alright, to find the man laying nearby with blood pouring from his temple.

"Zelig!" cried out Frost. He scrambled to his feet and darted over the rumbling ridge to the man, crouching down to hold his shoulders. He turned the man over carefully to examine the wound on his head.

Zelig murmured and lifted his hand to touch the gash and then flinched. Frost could not understand the sounds he was making. The man was speaking in his own language, not the few words of the Villagers that he had learnt. Frost wiped away some of the blood.

"You will be okay," he assured the long-haired man. "Such wounds bleed heavily, but it is not deep."

The man blinked and groaned.

"Come, we should get you home as soon as we can."

Frost scoured the rocks for the bags and belongings that had been scattered when the land was turned, stuffing them all back into one carry bag, and then helped the man climb to his feet and then offered a shoulder for him to lean on. Together they walked slowly back down the ridgeline. Frost listened carefully to the voice of the mountain that growled far below his feet. Something was wrong. The few butterflies resting on the rocks didn't seem to have been disturbed by this last rush of stone, they remained exactly in their place.The mountain seemed angrier than it had before, but thankfully Frost and the visitor suffered no further injury by frustrated jabs from deep within the earth.

Before they left the rocky ground of the ridge, Frost sat Zelig down on a solid seeming boulder and knelt down to the path. He turned to face back along the mountain and lowered his hands to the ground. He closed his eyes.

Frost tried to listen for the mountain. It was hard to hear

now. He knew that he should still leave thanks to the mountain, for allowing them to leave, but he was angry that the mountain had hurt the visitor. He slowed his breathing and waited, until he felt that he could hear the rhythm of the mountain's heart. It was slower than the tide, but he could hear it.

He spoke a simple thanks to the mountain, and pulled out the dried fish he had brought with him. He left it on the path and then stood and helped Zelig move towards the grassy hills.

No rocks came to swim down with them. Frost could see them circling in the distance, watching the people struggling to move down the slopes. Frost thought that the distance was probably for the best. Zelig had seemed so tense and nervous around the rocks that the man would at least stay calm now.

The blood from Zelig's head had stopped flowing by the time they entered the forest, and Frost was able to call over a keeper, who made sure that the wound was clean.

"You have done well Frost," they told him. "But now he should probably return to his people. They will take care of him properly."

At the end of the forest, Zelig was holding his own weight again, instead of leaning heavily on Frost's shoulder. He paused and looked down at the young man.

"Thank you for your help," he said. He pulled his bag forward and withdrew the leaf block where he drew his Maps. He turned to the one he had made earlier in the day, showing the distant white spears and the valleys Frost had never been to. He knelt down and spent some time drawing the same symbols and shapes onto another of the leaves. Then he tore it out. He held up the thin material to Frost.

"Here. Keep this. As a way to say thanks."

Frost took the Map and looked at it. It was so strange to look at, but he understood the shapes more now after watching Zelig creating the map and pointing out the places he was including in it. Frost turned the leaf over, trying to work out where the top was. But how could the land have a top that wasn't the sky? He rolled the Map into a thin tube and tucked it into his carry bag. He would keep this treasure safe back inside his family's home. He bowed to Zelig.

"I am honoured."

VII. "LOST"

The next day the visitors arrived early and were standing patiently outside Frost's home when he woke.

"Good morning," he said to them, while rubbing at his eyes.

"Good morning! Would you take us back beyond the swimming hills?" asked Zelig. "We think there is much more for us to see here!"

"Certainly," agreed Frost. He got dressed and ate a simple breakfast, and then led the visitors through the village and towards the forest.

The tall woman, who Frost believed was called Berith, spoke to him as they walked.

"Zelig says land is changing?"

Frost frowned.

"What do you mean?"

"He say rocks moved slower, trees moved slower?" She tilted her head in a way that he recognised. She was asking a question.

"Maybe a little."

"This why we come back today." She nodded firmly. "Many lands change. We keep knowledge, so they remembered. Must act fast."

"Do the lands always change in every place you visit?" asked Frost softly.

Berith opened her mouth, but before she could reply they saw a large group of keepers standing outside the edges of the forest, crouching low and watching the trees. Frost saw his father amongst them.

"Is something wrong?" he asked Thunder.

"The trees. They seem sick."

"Sick?"

One of the visitors stepped forward. It was the one who had kept a twig, the shifting man. Frost thought he might be called Luter. "There is something wrong? May I know?"

Frost's father frowned but nodded. He pointed at the trees, and Frost looked closer. A breeze lifted and Frost could hear the way it pushed as the trees, and caused their thin leaves to rustle. The wind passed and the trees slowed and stopped.

"They aren't moving?" Frost was shocked.

"They move some. But they are slow, and they are not paying attention to us."

"Can we travel through the forest?" asked Frost. He was worried that he would disappoint these explorers in their search for more knowledge.

"You can, but carefully. We do not know why they have changed their behaviour, and we do not know if they will be dangerous. I will send a keeper with you."

Frost introduced the keeper, whose name meant the glow of a summer sunset reflected on the ocean, to the visitors. Ocean reached out his hand, palm facing the visitors. They lifted theirs and patted his palm with their own, each taking a turn and then stepping aside for the others. Ocean glanced at Frost who shrugged. The visitors had been told what to do, but they did not understand. Frost knew that it was not intended to be insulting. Ocean bowed to them, and they bowed in response, but Frost touched Ocean's shoulder so that he would not grow angry.

Together they moved along the path into the forest. Frost could see what his father meant. There were still some trees moving, but they were slow and aimless. They moved across the path, and Frost was nearly knocked down more than once. Ocean kept a close eye on the visitors, ensuring that they were not taken by surprise. Luter watched the trees with his mouth hanging wide open.

"Why this?" he asked.

"We do not know," answered Ocean. "We were discussing it outside, trying to understand what has happened."

"Is something wrong? Poison?"

Ocean shook his head. "We don't know if this is right or wrong. We have no stories of this happening before, but perhaps it is how forests are meant to be?"

Frost tried to help interpret Ocean's words for the visitors. Zelig's face scrunched up. Frost knew enough to see that he was not satisfied by Ocean's answer.

When they emerged from the slow and stilted forest, Frost clutched his hands to his stomach.

The hills were motionless.

Frost and the visitors walked slowly out onto the grass beneath the hills and looked around them. The hills were still and there was no sign of movement along the mountain ridge behind them. There were no butterflies fluttering between the flowers in the grass.

"What is this? Where have dancing stones gone?" asked one of the visitors.

Frost felt fear clutch at his heart. Where had they gone? First the trees ceased their endless swarming over and under one another, and now the stones sat still on hills that looked as though they had never moved at all. He felt as though he were looking into a rockpool filled with empty shells and discarded fish heads, left by an uncaring fisherman.

Ocean met the young boy's eyes. "We should go back and tell Coal."

Frost didn't know how to respond. He took another step forward and lifted a hand, as though the sight before him was a picture in the sky that he could press through and tear down. But it was not. Ocean stepped up behind him.

"Frost? We should take them back."

Frost nodded.

The keeper led them quickly through the lethargic forest and then explained what they had seen to the other keepers who were still gathered at the other end of the path. Frost's father came to him to ask what he had seen.

"Ocean explained it true, the hills are sleeping." Frost couldn't bring himself to describe the land in another way. They must be asleep, and they would wake and dance again soon.

"Do they sleep like the mountain?"

Frost knew what his father meant. The mountain slept fitfully, and dreamed, and it tossed and turned while it dreamed. Thunder wanted to know what signs of life the hills were giving to Frost. Frost opened his mouth but could think of no words. Finally he closed his jaw and shook his head.

"Come, you will need to describe what you saw," said Thunder.

Frost was led to Coal. The visitors came too. The conversation was too fast for them to keep up, though they tried to explain what they could when asked a direct question. Frost was led forward and stood in the middle of a wide circle of people and explained the sights he had seen, the gently waving branches of the forest, the heavy solidness of the hillsides.

After he had spoken, and the visitors and Ocean had given their own agreeing statements, the visitors asked if they could return to their skyboat and their captain, the man with the rectangular beard. They said that they needed to let him know what they had seen as well. Berith's brow was creased and she kept her eyes lowered.

Frost went home and sat in the middle of the house, looking at his hands. What had happened to the land? Why would it fall asleep now? What has changed?

"It is the visitors," declared his younger sister as she came into the house.

"What?"

"They have done something to the land, can't you see?" She put her hands on her hips and looked down at him. "Everything was fine before they arrived."

"But they can't have, I've spent time with them," Frost protested. "They are curious and kind! They wouldn't do anything to hurt the land."

"The visitors have come back already," said Frost's father from the doorway. "They say they have an announcement."

The people of the village gathered on the beach beneath the skyboat. A breeze was blowing from the ocean. Frost shivered and wrapped his hands around himself to stave off the chill.

Once they were standing in a half circle on the beach, facing the ladder that extended down to the sand, the villagers became quiet. Coal stepped forward and addressed the visitors who were waiting. Only some of them were there.

"We hear you wish to speak with us. What do you have to say?"

The man with the rectangle beard, Gulrick, took one step closer and began to speak. He spoke in his own language but Frost could recognise some words in the speech. The man was clearly trying to show that he had learned something in his short time with the villagers so far, by using some of their language.

"Bad... Big... Us... Away..."

The words he recognised sounded dangerous. What had happened?

Justice stepped forward once Gulrick had finished talking.

"The visitors do not wish to insult your wonderful hospitality. However, they fear that they may have discovered something that will be a danger to yourselves, and your land."

A murmur ran through the crowd.

"From the stories you have shared with them, and the places you have introduced them to, they fear that your land is changing."

The villagers' whispers were different this time. Frost could tell by the tone that many of his friends and family were discussing the things that they had already seen for themselves. The slowing of the swarm would have been the center of conversation, he knew. Visions of green grassy hills, static and still, lingered in the back of his mind and Frost felt as though a shadow was passing over him. They were right. The land was changing.

"They have seen such things before, but now they fear that this change may have been caused by their arrival. Though they wished to visit and learn, they fear that something they brought with them will damage this place. And so they will go."

An empty silence spread as Justice finished. The sounds of the waves against the sand and breeze whistling by were all that could be heard. A rope slapped against the floating building, banging hollowly.

"Are they sure?" asked Coal eventually. Her voice seemed so small to Frost.

"No." Justice shook his head. "But they are not willing to risk you. I will leave with them."

"It is our custom to farewell our visitors properly."

"It cannot be this time. This must be a quick severing. It is as though they carry disease."

The villagers gasped. Frost stepped away from the visitors before he could think about what he was doing. Coal turned and made eye contact with some of the important members of the village. Then she squared her shoulders and turned back to Justice.

"Then it must be. We will not hold them here."

Justice spoke briefly to Gulrick, who nodded. Then they began climbing the rope ladder.

The villagers remained on the sand and watched as the last of the visitors climbed higher and higher, until they each climbed inside the building and the door closed behind them. The villagers watched, with their heads leaning back, as a humming noise began to emerge from the building. The sound grew louder and louder. Frost watched as the skyboat began to move, and the sight reminded him of where the rocks swum through the hills.

It spun slowly in place, until one end was pointed out across the white tipped waves, and then it began to push forward through the sky. None of the villagers moved from the beach until the building was a distant shape amongst the clouds, no more identifiable than a seagull.

Frost walked slowly up the beach with the others. Most of the villagers had their eyes upon the ground, and very few people were talking.

Ray came up beside him and slipped her hand into his.

"Are you alright?" she asked.

He nodded. "I am. But I know that what they were afraid of is true. Something has changed in the land."

She hummed in agreement and squeezed his fingers. Together they crested the dunes and walked back towards their home.

Frost spent a week returning to the hills, passing through the slowly shifting forest. The trees did not slow any further, and the keepers told him that they saw signs of promise. Small shoots were stretching up from the dark earth below the canopy, and the trees were hunching over them protectively.

The hills remained still during all this time. Frost walked heavily from one slope to the next, tracing his fingers across the boulders that lay motionless on their sides. He watched the empty fields rustle in the wind, wondering where the butter-flies might be.

After a week, Frost lay on the top of the nearest hill, feeling the grass tickling his hands and ears, and he watched the clouds cross the sky, in a silence that thrummed through his head.

That night, as he sat in his family's home, scooping his evening meal into his mouth, his mother leaned over and spoke to him.

"I would like to try and raise everyone's spirits tomorrow," she said. "And I will need some fruits and birds to make the most delicious meal."

"Do you need me to gather them for you?" asked Frost.

His mother nodded.

"Certainly. What do you need?"

"You will need to take a large bag," she said, listing off points on her fingers. "Half fill it with the red fruits that grow from the spiked tree on the far side of the ridge."

Frost nodded.

"And then I would like you to hunt three of the fat blue birds with the red eyes that often nest in these trees. There is a grove that often has these birds on the far side of the ridge. They live in the valley Tide's son dug as a path for his fishing boat. You will know the way by-"

But Frost had already stood up and returned his bowl to the side of the home, so that it could be cleaned out. He smiled at his mother.

"I will find it!"

Frost opened his box of treasures and rummaged through the important objects that he kept there. His father's fishing stone was wrapped in strong cord, waiting for the next time Frost intended to catch the biggest fish he had ever seen. A small toy, woven from thick leaves, that his sister had held tightly to while she was very small, was carefully moved to one side. And then, beneath these other things, Frost found where he had kept the Map.

He pulled the strange flat thing out of the box. It was curled up, like a broad flat pale leaf, with a copy of the drawing that the visitor had made on it. Frost had sat with the man and listened as he explained what it was, and how each line was a drawing of the real world, pulled down and placed onto the map so that others may study and learn from it though they never saw the land itself.

He touched one finger to the map and followed the line that meant the path through the forest. At the other side he moved his finger through the curves that meant the hills. Then he measured finger widths to the far side of the ridge, and the small marks that meant the forests and paths and valleys that the visitor had seen beyond. *There,* he said to himself, planting his finger on a spot beyond the spring valley. *That is where the fruits and birds will be.*

From where she sat near the fire behind him, Frost's grandmother, whose name means the yearning of a tree towards the sky, watched and said nothing.

TAONGA

The solid greenstone
of my mother's love
that I wore above my heart

The polished pounamu,
native interweaving
that was light around my neck

is broken.

THE ALTAR

For Sale: One Wedding Dress, Classic Style, Unworn, $700 ONO
ph (09) 668-7233

Wasps buzzed along the wooden fences of the street. Bees worked hard among the flowers and bushes clustered around the white-painted wooden gate outside the address Sarah had been given. She could just see one wasp eating a fat green caterpillar by the letterbox. The sun glowed through the windscreen of her Mirage as she sat and looked over the house. It burned the tip of her nose.

The other houses in the street stood beneath full leafed trees, but not this one. Instead dark green hedges squatted along every side. Only the dark grey tiles of the rook were visible over them with only the colour of the roses around the gate lightening the view. Beyond the roses, through the gate, Sarah could just make out a porch with a thin metal wind chime hanging over a wicker chair.

Sarah sighed and reached over to pick up her handbag, flinching from the heat off the vinyl seats, before getting out of the car. The air outside somehow felt even hotter and a lone bead of sweat worked its way from the ponytail bunched at the back of her head all the way down her spine, leaving a slightly uncomfortable trail on her skin.

Johnny had ducked his head around the kitchen doorway as he pulled on his work shirt that morning.

"I'm going to the pub with Todd after work, want to join us?"

"You know I can't drink at the moment," she had answered. There was an extra weight in her stomach that had nothing to do with her pregnancy.

"Yeah yeah, you could have a coke or something though," Johnny continued.

"There'd be all those smokers too. I can't risk that. We can't risk that." Sarah wondered if he even understood.

"I just thought it'd be nice to get you out of the house," he muttered, glaring at the floor.

"That would be lovely," Sarah smiled. For a moment she felt hope, like the shining sun peering through the kitchen curtains. "Why don't we go to a movie instead then?"

"The movies?" Johnny's shoulders slumped. "Yeah, I guess. I'll ask Todd if there's anything he wants to see."

"Couldn't it just be you and me honey?" Sarah asked.

Johnny stared at her for long seconds. She could see the curl on the edge of his lip and the slight narrowing of his dark irises and knew his reply before he spoke. She had already turned back to the dishes piled up beside the sink by the time he replied.

"I'll see you back here tonight Sarah. Don't wait up."

His footsteps echoed through the scarcely furnished flat as he walked to the front door. It had creaked open and slammed shut as he left.

THE SUN BEAMED down on Sarah as she walked up the narrow gravel path to the house. She could hear a rumbling that rose and fell in the distance, the sound of car engines driving down nearby streets. The peacefulness of the place made her smile.

Seen up close the painted walls of the house weren't as bright as they had seemed. Faint cracks stretched across the surface like a rich and vain old woman's wrinkles. Sarah could see where the colour had faded after decades of sunlight. A thick cottony wad of spider web sprouted from the ceiling of the porch, wedged into the corner above the door. As Sarah studied it, a shudderingly large spider crawled out and lazily moved over to munch on a bee that was well-wrapped in white strands of web. Sarah swallowed and wiped her hands on her hips.

With her eyes fixed firmly on the small stained-glass window attempting to enliven the front door, Sarah pushed on the doorbell. From somewhere inside the house a chime sounded, like the tinkling of tiny bells. Moments later the door swung open.

A dark figure stood in the gloomy hall within, flashing eyes staring back at her.

Sarah started back before the figure stepped forward into the sunlight, revealing a short rounded old man in neat warm clothes. He squinted up at her through his small thick spectacles.

"Good morning my dear! My name is Mr Winslow; please

do feel free to call me Arnold however. I assume you must be Sarah?" He scrunched his nose, shifting the spectacles higher for a better focus.

"Yes, that's right. I called you this morning." She held out a hand and tried on her brightest retail-worker smile.

"I remember." He took her hand in his soft fingers and shook it. "May I just say, you are even prettier than your lovely voice had led me to expect. My, but you do look so much like my dear Annie." He looked into Sarah's blue eyes with his small gray ones and smiled. "Do come in."

SARAH HADN'T BOTHERED to finish washing the dishes after Johnny had left. She had sat in the torn chair beside the small table squeezed into the corner of the kitchen and stared at the grease-crusted pile from last night's dinner, stacked haphazardly at one end of the kitchen bench. Grains of rice floated in bowls of water. The sun shone past unruly bushes clutching to the outside wall of the unit she and Johnny had begun renting two weeks earlier. A hint of its warmth reached Sarah where she sat, idly flipping through the mail.

All the envelopes had already been torn open, but Sarah didn't check the contents of any of them. Instead she stood and went to the cupboard for two slices of fresh-ish bread out of a half-empty bag that was decorated, for some reason, with a smiling butterfly. She put the slices into the toaster and pushed the level down with a loud click.

In the middle of the kitchen table sat a small wire frame bowl that held a few bruised bananas and a couple of apples no-one seemed to want. Simple flexible magnets plastered small sheets of paper to the fridge. Sarah thought the magnets felt like greasy rubber.

One was at her eye level as she stood, waiting for her toast.

It was a wedding invitation. This was clear from the silver bells and white ribbon that decorated the paper. It cordially invited, on behalf of their parents, the friends and family of Sarah Vernon and Jonathan Glasgow to join the happy couple for their magical day (RSVP).

The others papers worthy of fridge space were less inviting. Instead they spoke in the precise clipped sentences of a company that could now promise violence instead of merely insinuating. They looked like they were trying to shoulder the invitation off the fridge entirely.

The bushes outside the window wore a powder-blue dusting of pale tiny flowers. Sarah watched the bees hover erratically between the minute petals, rummaging for what traces of pollen they could scrape together in the hopes of building their honeycombs and creating their hives. She had eaten her toast dry, in silence.

Mr Winslow's hallway was narrow and dim, which surprised Sarah. The garden and outside of the house were so large and well-lit by the sun that she had expected the inside to be the same. She almost had to bend over to avoid bumping her head on the dangling, unlit light shades. Mr Winslow placed a hand on the small of her back as he guided her through a door on the right and into a Spartan sitting room at the rear of the house. She felt her skin shiver at the feel of his hand pressing her damp shirt against the skin of her back.

There was a single smudged window in the room, looking out into a backyard that held only a rusty washing line. The line grew from a weed-choked concrete pad. The lawn was long and golden with unchecked dandelions. The sides of the yard were rimmed by crumbling grey brick walls.

"Why is the front garden so much prettier?" Sarah found herself asking.

Mr Winslow glanced at her over his shoulder. His eyes shimmered from the tiny circles of his spectacles as he answered her. "For the bees, my dear. They seem to love my work. Now, please take a seat. I'll make you a cup of tea. How do you like it?"

"Just a small drop of milk. No sugar, thank you," she said as she settled onto the small sofa that crouched by the only other door in the room. It was only in marginally better condition than the furnishings she and Johnny had begun gathering for their flat.

"Not much of a sweet tooth, eh? My Annie was never one for sugar either." He chuckled. "She always said she was sweet enough."

He pottered through the door next to the sofa and Sarah craned her neck to see what was beyond. She saw a tiny fridge, the white smearing into a pale grey, before the door swung shut. The sound of Mr Winslow clattering through the cupboards was muted by the wall.

After a moment Sarah stood up to explore the room. Everything was old and fading. The wall opposite her held a mantelpiece above a boarded up fireplace. On it was a black-and-white photo of a couple, set in a golden frame. The glass over the photo was thick with smeary fingerprints. The man appeared to be smiling, but the woman's mouth appeared set in a grim horizontal line. She sat in front of the man. Sarah wondered if this was Annie.

SARAH HAD FINISHED her toast and decided to clean the flat. She didn't relish the argument that would occur if Johnny came home to the same dishes from the morning. Soon she had washed off all the old Indian food and dried them with a Christmas Carol dishcloth that her aunty had given her for Easter, and put them away. She held her left hand against the bench and swept the crumbs from her toast into it so she could dump them into the sink as the dishwater drained.

Finally she stood in front of the fridge for five minutes, without focusing on the large underlined lettering that glared from the notes on its surface, wishing there was something more interesting to eat inside it than the yellowing broccoli and processed cheese slices. She got as far as opening the fridge door before changing her mind and switching on the kettle for a cup of tea.

She held the mug in both hands and let the heat of the tea seep through her fingers and up her arms to her shoulders. Then she moved to the lounge with its worn out comfy chairs and settled down, lifting her feet up to tuck them under her bottom. She didn't bother to turn on the TV seeing as it would have involved getting up and fiddling with the slightly bent bunny-ear antennae sitting on top of the set in order to watch the thrilling daytime combination of soft focus soap operas and infomercials.

The flat had felt very quiet.

"THERE YOU ARE."

Sarah flinched. Winslow was standing behind her with a steaming cup of tea. He blinked at her through his spectacles. She tried to smile at him and took the tea, murmuring a thank you.

"Is that you and Annie?" She asked, pointing to the photo with her little finger, as she was holding the teacup in both hands.

"Yes actually, it is. You can see the resemblance between the two of you, can't you?"

Sarah frowned. The woman in the photo had short, wavy dark hair and full cheeks. She could feel her blonde ponytail brushing between her shoulder blades.

"Uh... Yes. Yes, I see it." Sarah sipped at her tea instead of looking at Winslow. The dark liquid swirled between her hands.

"I am glad," said Winslow, his lightly wrinkled face creasing further as he smiled. "It's something about the eyes I imagine. It so often is."

"Yeah," Sarah moved away from him to stand by a tall thin coffee table. "So, is Annie home?"

"Oh no," answered Winslow. "I haven't seen Annie for many, many years."

"Oh. I'm sorry. I assumed that the two of you were... well..."

"We were planning on getting married you see. The dates had been set, our guests had been invited, and everything was prepared." He sat down in a tatty armchair beside the unused fireplace and near the window. He looked very small. "She left me standing at the altar though."

"How awful!" Sarah stepped closed to him without meaning to, but his lips twitched towards a smile and he waved her away.

"It all happened a long time ago now. I guess it just goes to show that you can never be sure how well you know another person. Even someone you may love very dearly."

"I think Johnny and I know each other pretty well by now. We've been together for a few years. We just moved in together."

"Yes, that should help somewhat," agreed Winslow. "Of course, that wasn't really an option for Annie and me." He sniffed and pulled a handkerchief from his sleeve to rub his nose. "Tell me Sarah, why are you looking for a wedding dress? I mean, you say you two have moved in together anyway?" He tucked the handkerchief back into his sleeve but never took his eyes off Sarah.

Sarah blushed and put a hand on her stomach. "It doesn't really make much difference I know, but I talked to Johnny about it and we agreed that we'd like our baby to be born into a proper family."

"I understand. Annie and I had a similar deadline ourselves."

"Oh," said Sarah. She couldn't think of anything better. She found herself looking at the mantelpiece and the walls, searching for a photo of Winslow's children. She didn't find any. She sipped her tea and wondered what to say. Did you never meet your baby then?

"Nearly finished," asked Winslow, slapping his hands onto his knees. "I'd better show you this dress then, shouldn't I?"

He stood and motioned her into the hallway again. She finished her tea and put the cup down on the coffee table and followed him. There were no windows in the hall. There was a picture in a frame on the wall opposite her as she walked out but she couldn't make it out in the gloom. She had an impression of elaborate architecture, like a cathedral, and then Winslow had ushered her into a small bedroom.

SARAH HAD CAREFULLY DRAWN a thick black line around the ad with her vivid marker while Johnny had been in the shower. Four other circles slowly leaked their ink through the cheap newspaper pages, as well as a few that had been meticulously crossed out. One had been scribbled over so heavily that the ink must have stained at least ten layers of newsprint beneath.

The smell of bread cooking into golden toast wafted under

her nose and she sat back in her aluminium frame chair. She put down the vivid and flexed the fingers of her right hand and then rubbed her eyes with her thumb and forefinger. Just before the bread began to turn into charcoal the toaster popped up. Sarah stood up and walked over to the bench to pick it out and then slouched against the stainless steel bench top that surrounded the sink and stared out the window. The sun was just rising outside and a few cars were already on the road, in a tired but optimistic attempt to beat the morning traffic rush.

She put the toast on a plate and spread a thin layer of butter on it.

Behind her Johnny walked in the door hall door and put his arms around her waist, resting his hands together on her belly. He leaned over to kiss her cheek his lips lightly brushing against her skin. She smiled and leaned into him, sliding the plate towards him. As he picked up the toast and bitten into it, their eyes had met and Sarah had felt warmth fill her from within.

THE WALLPAPER WAS an unsettling light red with a pattern that seemed to be floral. There was a small window near the roof that didn't let in much light. Sarah felt like she was in a box and found herself breathing quickly. Above the bed hung a large portrait of the woman from the photo in the lounge; at least she was smiling in this painting.

Winslow straightened the duvet and fussed with a few bits and pieces on top of a dresser and murmured for Sarah to come further in. She couldn't help feeling her skin crawl as she stepped nearer to the painted woman.

The small man pushed the pillows higher against the headboard. "Just take a seat and I'll fetch the dress."

As Sarah sank into the soft mattress, Winslow hurried past her and lit a short fat candle on the bedside table. Then he scurried around to do the same on the other side of the bed.

He saw her expression and laughed as he waved out the second match and placed it on the tray the candle sat in.

"It gets awfully musty in this house, particularly this little room here," he explained. "I find the scent helps me relax."

Sarah nodded and shifted on the bed. She had to look away for a moment as she got comfortable but when she turned back to Winslow she saw he was staring at the painting above her, his lips moving rapidly. It looked as though he mouthed the word "Annie" but she couldn't make out anything else before he saw her watching and stopped. He rushed over to the bedroom's cupboard.

He opened the door and hunched down to rummage through the objects inside. Before long he had removed a selection of dusty containers and was sliding out a long flat box. He stood it upright against the wall beside the cupboard without turning to face Sarah and began to lift the lid.

JOHNNY HAD SLIPPED into the kitchen chair with a glass of juice. "So, what have you got planned to keep you busy today then?" he asked between sips.

"Nothing much." Now Sarah was leaning with her back to the bench. She filled a glass with water and took a sip. "I thought I'd go and check out an ad I found in the paper. It's another second hand wedding dress."

Johnny picked at the small flakes of plastic that were peeling away from the table's surface with his left hand. He took another sip of his juice, swallowed and licked his lips before commenting.

"Sarah," he began and then paused, searching for words.

He lifted his gaze to the ceiling. A single fly was walking upside-down near the light bulb and Johnny watched it for a while. Sarah patiently waited for him to gather his thoughts, though tiny creases appeared in the skin around her eyes. "Sarah," he tried again. "I know we have to make do for a lot of things for our wedding. As cheap a venue as we can find in time, whoever can do the best price on a few flowers, all of that sort of thing. Obviously that hasn't left a lot of money spare for "luxury items"." He slotted the finger quotes into place casually. "But your dress should be special shouldn't it? I mean, maybe we could cut back on groceries for a month and just live on rice flavouring or something? Maybe we could go and talk to the bank? We might be able to get another loan."

Sarah had been thrilled at his suggestion. But, eventually they had argued, and he had left. Then she had called the number on the ad. The gentle voice at the other end had confirmed that he had an unworn second-hand wedding dress for sale and had happily provided a time and address, before chiding her to take her time.

"Sarah," he said, not looking at her. "I'm afraid I lied to you."

"What do you mean? Did Annie not leave you?"

"Oh no, she left. I lied in the ad. The dress has been worn before." He moved the lid aside to reveal a stunning white wedding gown, delicately embroidered and torn open across the belly, caked with thick black dried blood at the neck and stomach. Sarah opened her mouth to scream but no noise escaped.

Winslow's spectacles flared in the faint light from the candles as he turned and hid his eyes. The knife in his hand sheened.

"It's always the same with you girls," he hissed. "Getting

pregnant just so you can trap some man and squash his youth and his ambitions." He looked over Sarah's head to the painting on the wall, wreathed in smoke from the candles.

"She won't get away with it Annie. I won't let you do it to someone else."

Outside, between the sweet roses that grew in the front garden, bees moved serenely beneath the warm sun.

TRIPTYCH

Chapel full of candles.
White flowers at the end of the pews.
Everyone's clothes have been ironed.
Two youths, with eyes like mirrors,
Speak promises at the altar.

Rain washes it away.

House full of shadows.
Dirty dishes are piled in the sink.
Everyone's laundry in a pile.
Two humans, with eyes like furnaces,
Hurl regrets in the hallway.

Rain washes it away.

Cemetery full of memories.
Bouquets are placed on each grave.

Everyone's clothes are black.
One mourner, with eyes like rivers,
Says farewells in their heart.

Rain washes it away.

ORPHANS

ORIGINALLY PUBLISHED IN NOCTURNE
MAGAZINE (NZ) ISSUE 2

Mary shivered and stared into the wood burner. The dying embers of last night's fire winked back at her like tiny glowing eyes. She tugged her white fluffy dressing gown tighter around herself and reached into the wood box. Nothing.

Damn it. Why didn't Steve chop more wood yesterday?

She snorted, walked out of the living room and down the short hall to the front door. A small wire shoe rack sat next to it and a pair of gumboots lay on the linoleum. As she bent over to pick them up Mary's eyes caught sight of the small, pink-edged sneakers that were hiding beneath a pair of Steve's work boots. She paused.

With a deep breath she shook herself and grabbed the gumboots. Within moments she had opened the door and stepped outside, hopping as she tugged on the boots.

The house sat in a shallow bowl surrounded by fields. In summer the hills around them shone like an emerald sea and animals dotted the landscape with movement. Distant power lines stilted from hilltop to hilltop on their way to town, five kilometres away. In summer Mary would stand at the top of the four concrete steps that led to her front door and felt as though she could see the whole world laid out in front of her.

It was not summer now. It was barely even spring.

All the worst parts of winter still lingered on. The beating rain and sudden winds. The icy cold. And the fog.

The fog this morning was thick and heavy, dampening the world with its weight. Mary found that she could barely see the path at the bottom of the steps and only a fraction of the lawn past it. The wooden fence that divided her home from the fields was completely invisible. Everything was white.

From that tiny glimpse of grass, Mary could see that the dew had frozen. Each blade stood stiffly, the deep green muted into pastel by the thin layer of ice. I should've found my gloves. Mary held her hands together in front of her mouth and huffed into them for warmth. She rubbed them as she set off on the narrow path around the house, heading for the woodshed.

Her breath was visible in a shifting cloud in front of her and it made her smile. This is crazy, she told herself as she stretched her arms out. I can only just make out the walls of the house and it's right next to me!

Her shin connected sharply with something on the path. Ow! What on earth was that? In order to see it properly she had to lean down. On the side of the path, huddling against the house, was a small tricycle. The painted frame shone beneath the dew. Metallic streamers hung limply from the handlebars.

Mary's throat felt thick. She swallowed with difficulty. Her eyes felt hot, even in the crisp air of the morning. Lips firmly pressed together, she grabbed the tricycle and heaved it into the fog, away from the house. Mercifully, the fog swallowed the tricycle without judgement but the crash of the tricycle hitting the fence seemed to linger in her ears. Mary realised her shoulders were hunched. She carefully straightened up and rubbed her face with the heels of her hands before continuing down the path.

Through the fog ahead of her, a dark shape began to appear. In front of it a skeletal tree seemed to materialise all at once, trailing the fog through its thick-jointed branches. She walked past the tree and was standing in front of the looming shape. It was the woodshed. From somewhere in the shrouded fields nearby came the deep mournful sound of a cow.

There were plenty of ringed log sections heaped in the shed, but almost no chopped wood. An axe was buried head-first into a section of wood lying flat on the floor. The axe crunched out as she tugged on the handle. At least this one sounds fairly dry. Most of this wood must be sodden by now. You'd think he would get this stuff sorted earlier, after all we've been living out here for four years now. Mary found herself thinking of small sneakers. Maybe not this winter though.

She shifted her grip around the wood and heard a cow lowing from outside. The sound cut off abruptly. Mary paused and peered out into the silent white emptiness of the fog. What was that?

Part of the fog shifted, as if in a faint breeze. Mary's hand tightened around the wooden handle and she leaned out of the woodshed door. The fog stifled everything like a cobweb curtain, insubstantial but impenetrable. Every stark black branch of the tree stood out against the white as it jutted precisely into the damp air. Behind the tree some of the fence was visible for a few metres before it faded away.

"Steve?" If that little bastard has snuck home then I'll...

An organic noise squelched through the mist. It came from the field over the fence.

Mary lifted the axe in both hands and crunched through the stiff grass. She squinted and tried to peer into the bright gloom. That almost sounded like a foot in the mud, but why did it only take one step? She tried not to think about the fact that the milking sheds were far away on the other side of the house. There was no reason for Steve to be in that field.

"Is someone there?" In the field the fog swirled, a curling tongue of mist that slowed, stilled and vanished. "I have an axe," she blustered, feeling foolish as soon as the words left her mouth.

A faint sound reached her, too quiet to properly make out, but repetitive. She rolled her shoulders then clambered over the fence, pausing only to disentangle her dressing gown from splinters in the wood.

The sound tickled her ears as she slowly moved through the thick mud. She placed her feet carefully to avoid slipping and making a sudden noise. Her heart was thudding high in her chest.

Quickly the fence disappeared behind her. It was like the world had been torn away and now all that was left was herself, the uprooted earth wet beneath her gumboots and the insubstantial cloak of the fog.

And her axe. The wood felt reassuringly real against her skin.

Slowly something emerged from the fog in front of her. It was a dim shape, low against the ground. The soft sound was coming from it. Now that she was this close, Mary could hear it better. It was a snuffling sort of sound, like a little girl with a runny nose.

Mary lifted the axe higher in front of her and edged forward. The shape developed a dull, brown leathery texture. Suddenly she recognised what it was. It was a cow. But what's wrong with it? A cow shouldn't be lying on its side like this. Was it this cow that went quiet?

Something moved behind the cow.

Mary nearly bit her tongue. "Hey! Hey, who's there?" she

yelped. Whatever it was, it began to shuffle around from the far side of the cow. Mary released the breath she didn't realise she'd been holding. It's just a calf.

There was something immensely grounding about the calf. Just the sight of it reminded Mary that the world was still around her, even if it was out of sight for the moment. She smiled as the calf tottered towards her on its spindly adolescent legs. It looked at her with gigantic wet brown eyes and made its wheezy snuffling noise again.

"Its alright sunshine. You're going to be just fine. Now, what do you say we try to figure out what's happened here?" She rubbed the calf's head and let the axe dangle from one hand as she strolled over to the cow. What she found made her retch.

Settle down lady, you've seen worse at the meatworks. But the shock of the sight had worked its way through her bones and she shuddered as she took another look.

The cow had been torn open. Its throat was a messy red wound and there were pieces of flesh and organs steaming on the ground beside the ragged split in its belly. The calf left Mary's side and muzzled its mother's head. Mary felt anger warm her blood as she watched.

"Okay you cowards! There are no wild animals around here, nothing that could do something this... this... Sick!" She spat the word. "I don't care if you show yourself or not, I'm calling the cops." With that she turned and began to mush her way back towards where she hoped the fence would be.

A curl of fog wisped past from behind her. The calf squealed. Mary spun around and gasped.

In the fog behind the dead cow, a few specks of red were drifting in the air. Is there a fire somewhere? No, wait... Mary realised the specks couldn't be hot ash or floating embers. They weren't drifting, they were moving sedately towards her.

Mary ran over to stand by the calf and found it trembling. She lifted the axe and watched as two tall figures solidified around the red flecks.

They were both at least a foot taller than her and incredibly pale. Mary found it hard to tell where their ivory skin finished and the fog began. They were humanoid shaped but impossibly thin. Their eyes blazed red, almost glowing, and their hair spiked in short tufts backwards from their sharp faces like flames frozen in place. They were naked.

"Who are?!" Mary stared. "WHAT are you?!"

They didn't answer. Instead they glanced at each other and smiled. One of them turned back to her and raised his arm to point a bony finger the calf. Mary felt her skin freezing. His hand was smeared with blood.

The creature opened his mouth and said something in a sibilant language that she couldn't understand. Inside his mouth she could see his deep red tongue, sliding across porcelain teeth. He stepped closer.

"No!" She yelled and swung the axe at waist height. He was still far enough away that the axe came nowhere near him. He watched Mary with his head tilted like an inquisitive bird. Mary stared into his swirling blood-red irises.

"No. You can't have her."

His eyes narrowed. The second figure crossed his arms and stepped backwards, hissing through grinning teeth. The first took another step forward, his smile fading. Mary stepped in front of the calf and hefted the axe.

"I said no. She's mine and I won't let you take her."

The figure kept moving and Mary could see shift of wiry muscles beneath his skin. The mist glistened wetly on him. He growled like a feral dog and lunged. Mary swung.

The axe felt heavy and ponderous as she pushed it through the air. The figure's pale hands stretched towards her eyes, curling like talons. His eyes glowed like molten iron. And then the blade of the axe slammed into his arm.

He screamed like a hawk as the metal moved easily through his pale flesh and sailed on to crunch into the side of his face. Momentum carried him forward to tumble in the mud beside Mary, tugging the axe out of her grasp. She could feel her heart pulsing and her hands shaking. Huh. No blood. She surprised herself with the calm way she surveyed the body. I'm probably in shock. From the corner of her eyes she saw a flicker of movement and snapped her head up.

The other creature was walking slowly in a wide circle around her. He didn't look as though he was angry, but he had stopped smiling. Mary started panting as she fumbled with the axe handle, eventually closing her eyes and planting a foot on the dead thing's neck so she could wrench the axe free. She was almost sobbing as she moved to stand between the calf and the second figure.

"I said no! I don't know what will happen to me for killing him," she wailed, jerking her head in the corpse's direction. "But do you know what? I don't care!" She took a deep tremulous breath and glared at the other figure. It stopped stalking across the mud and returned her gaze. She spoke through clenched teeth.

"You. Can't. Take. Her."

The world was still, swaddled in mist and silence. Somewhere there were cities and cars, coffee and radios, and people living out bright lives. But for Mary all of the world existed in the fog. The cold mud, her tiny calf, a tall pale stranger.

And her axe.

The figure took a step backwards and nodded at her. A hissing noise rose like a soft rain. At first she thought it came from the creature but it seemed to be coming from everywhere at once. Mary moved her head slowly, looking around in the fog. Glimpses of red faded in and out, deep in the white that enveloped the creature and her. The calf whined.

Then the figure nodded once more and walked away, melting into the fog. The hissing sound slowly faded along with his glowing eyes. Mary sank to her knees in the mud and put her arm over the calf, still clutching the axe tightly. The body of the creature she had killed dissipated like the clouds of her breath. She was alone.

Steve trudged home for lunch. The fog had nearly completely lifted and the sun was directly overhead but he was confused to find no sign of Mary in the house. He wandered outside to look for her.

"Mary? Mary, where are..." His voice died in his throat. Something was slumped in the field. He ran over, praying that everything was alright.

Mud covered Mary to her waist, ruining her favourite dressing gown and she had gone pale with the cold. The skin around her eyes was red and her cheeks were damp with tears, but she looked up at him with a smile. As he knelt down and held her close he heard her whisper through chattering teeth.

"I saved her. I didn't let them take her."

They sat in the mud with the calf as the sun slowly warmed the world again. Tiny green buds were appearing on the tree by the woodshed. Summer was coming.

DEPARTURE

Walking away across a sterile carpet
he approaches automatic doors
that will cut me off.

All I want is to call his name
and see his face again,
but my throat is too tight.

Next to me a woman murmurs
"Say: bye bye Grandad."
and the baby in her arms waves.

I try to put Grandad on the memory of his face,
slip an old-man mask on his departing figure.
It doesn't fit but I can't get it off again.

I don't know if the slick suit he wears is his
or who gave him that weathered briefcase,
and the lack of knowledge itches.

I want to take his hand and look into his eyes
to see who is inside,
hold him close until everything he is, is me.
But I just raise my hand in farewell.

Rictus smiles cover the faces of strangers
who all have their own reasons to cry
as he slips behind a partition
and is gone.

THE BABY WAS CRYING

Lloyd swum to consciousness from the watery depths of sleep, blinking and gasping as though he really had been underwater. He lay in the dark, calming his breath and pulse. On the bedside table, the monitor crackled as the baby's wail echoed from it. With a great effort of will and a long suffering sigh, Lloyd managed to push his legs out the side of the bed and onto the floor. He took a deep breath and sat up. From there he heaved himself to his feet and grabbed his phone from where it was charging on the nightstand. He pressed the button to activate the screen as he headed off down the hallway, facing it down so that he could see where he was going.

2.18am. Wonderful. Jackson still wasn't managing to sleep for much more than three hours before waking up. Lloyd gently opened the door to the baby's room, slipping his phone into his pocket, and slunk inside. The boy's cries pressed against his temples like fingers, jabbing. He moved towards the cot with his hands outstretched, feeling for the wooden railing. There was a small bang as he found it, and Lloyd flinched. The crying did not shift in intensity, so maybe he would be able to settle Jackson down in spite of the noise. Blind in the dark, he leaned over it.

"Shush now," he murmured over and over, as he reached down and stroked his son's shoulders gently. "Hush now, back to sleep." After a minute or two the cries calmed down and Jackson gurgled a little before falling back to the silence of sleep. Carefully, Lloyd lifted the blankets to cover more of the boy then backed away, keeping his hands behind him so he didn't back into the wall. Once outside, he drew the door closed with barely a click.

"I'm really getting the hang of this," he thought to himself as he started to walk back down the hall to his own room.

Just before his room, he noticed a light peeking from under a crack in the doorway to the living room. Curious, he pushed the door open and leaned inside. His wife Amy was sitting in one of the easy chairs, with her back to him.

"Good evening sweetheart," said Lloyd. "Why are you out of bed at this time in the morning?"

"I just got up to try and settle Jackson," said Amy with a smile as she turned to speak to her husband. "But he was so upset I decided to feed him."

Lloyd's felt ice shoot through his veins when he saw their baby boy Jackson happily breast feeding there in his mother's arms. He pressed the tips of his fingers together, remembering how he had reached down to soothe the wailing shape in the crib. Those fingertips burned as though he had jammed them into hot coals. From behind him, through the half open door of his bedroom, he heard the hissing of the baby monitor. The crying began again.

AN EXPENSIVE JACKET

On a still and bright February morning, while sitting outside the Brilliant Moon café at a small circular table that only wobbled very slightly, Kate Thomson exploded. This came as something of a shock to her boyfriend Steven Tanner who had just sat down opposite her with his cappuccino. He blinked twice and examined the clear goo that was pooling on the table between the tiny vase with two blue flowers in it on one side and the salt shaker on the other.

"How odd," he murmured. "She's never done that before." He reached for one of the napkins on the table but paused when he noticed thick drops slipping from it as he lifted it off the pile. "And I'm fairly sure that she didn't used to have quite so much mucus inside her. Blood seems much more traditional. I hope they don't think I'll pay for the cleaning."

A waitress gusted past Steven on her way to bestow a plate of pancakes upon some other table before swooping around to return to the dark space of the kitchen.

"Excuse me, miss?" called Steven. She managed to go from

"Striding Away" to "Standing Next To The Table" with a speed that made him jump. Her eyes stared blankly to a point slightly behind his head from above a smile that split her face horizontally.

"Goodmorningsir, whatcanIgetforyou?"

Steven took a moment to translate her speech in his head. "You see, it's just that my girlfriend appears to have exploded and I -"

"Was it squids?" the waitress asked, still smiling through his head.

"What? No! No, it wasn't squids. We were just sitting here quietly when -"

"Yeah, probably squids." The waitress nodded once with a sharp jerking motion. "I've never trusted them. Too shiny."

Steven's mouth hung open while he tried to process her contribution to the conversation. "Look, it has nothing to do with any sort of marine invertebrate, alright? I just wanted some dry napkins please."

"Why?"

Steven wiped his face, which had the unfortunate effect of slathering his hand in gobs of the clear goo that had hitherto covered his cheeks and forehead. The waitress hadn't blinked since he had called her over and he felt his eyes beginning to water in sympathy.

"Why? Because I'm covered in mucus and I'd quite like to clean my jacket. It cost a fair bit."

The waitress flicked her gaze down his dripping clothes and back up to stare past his face. "I'm sorry sir, that has nothing to do with us. Patrons seated in the Open Space are permitted to indulge in activities that would not be allowed inside but must remain personally responsible to others."

"What does that mean?"

"It means "In all cases of complaints please refer to the menu.""

Steven looked at the tabletop in front of him. There were two cups of coffee that would remain undrunk, which he considered an appalling waste of good money, an ashtray in the shape of a dolphin (for the nature lovers Steven supposed), the miniature flower display and a pair of salt and pepper shakers shaped like crabs.

"I don't have a menu."

The waitress said nothing. Steven sighed. "Could I have a -" The waitress pulled a rectangle of laminated cardboard from her apron and held it three inches from Steven's face. "-menu. Please." He took the menu and looked over it.

At the very bottom, in type so small that it almost looked like someone had dribbled ink along the page, was a note saying "Complaints? Call 022 416 3122". Steven squelched his hand into his trouser pocket and removed his cellphone. It was damp but not waterlogged. Steven closed his eyes and said "Oh god, please let my phone work."

"God doesn't work like that."

"What?"

"God is a force of infinite love and compassion that penetrates all objects. You can't change what is by wishing it so in his name."

Steven stared at the waitress as, apart from the last statement, she had not previously demonstrated that she was anything other than a well disguised robot.

"Besides, god is a title; it doesn't specify the deity you are attempting to invoke."

"I'm going to use my phone now. Please stop talking."

Steven dialled the number. The phone rang twice. Then there was a click as the other end connected and a pre-recorded male voice said "Life's not fair. Deal with it." then hung up. A trickle of slime bubbled out of the phone and down the inside of Steven's sleeve. It was surprisingly cold. He put the phone back in his pocket.

"That wasn't very helpful," he told the waitress.

"I blame the squids frankly."

"Will you stop talking about squids!?"

"Well how do you like that," she huffed, spun on her heel and began to walk away.

"Wait!" Steven held out an imploring hand. "I need your help! Please, before anything else can happen, you have to help me!" He plucked at the damp sleeve of his shirt around his wrist. "Please can I have some napkins? This jacket was very expensive."

"Before anything else can happen? I don't know what you think you're implying but we would never employ a squid!" The waitress glared at him and stalked inside.

Steven sighed and looked at his untouched cappuccino. This is so unfair, he thought. This jacket might spoil. Then he saw a scrap of cloth from Kate's clothes on the table beneath a shining coat of goop. And what happened to Kate? Steven ran his hands over his clothes to get rid of as much mucus as possible and stood up. And I'm certainly not leaving a tip after that service. I wonder if I can get a refund?

The street was quiet. A few elderly shoppers were looking through the window of a second-hand store while five real estate agencies loomed around them. Steven said good morning to the old ladies as he walked past, only for one of them to turn to the other and declare "I've always said there's something wrong with the youth of today." Steven blushed.

At the end of the row of shops, just past the entrance to a place called "Milligan's", was a small gravel car park where, acting in accordance with long established trends, Steven had parked his car. He had discovered previously that, if one carefully monitored the route of the traffic wardens, one could leave a car here for nearly two hours for free.

As he walked closer he pulled the alarm beeper out of his pocket. *I wonder if this works when stuffed full of translucent goo?* He never got the chance to find out as he found himself frozen in shock at the sight of the two squid standing on his car.

They were about five feet tall, from the triangular tip of their heads to the stretched out ends of their tentacles. Steven found himself furiously trying to figure out if they were hovering just high enough for their tentacles to graze his car, like some sort of googly-eyed, air-dwelling jellyfish; or if their tentacles were actually solid limbs, holding the body of the squid up like a tripod. The squid stared back at him with their unblinking saucer-sized eyes.

One lifted a paddle shaped flipper up to the glistening beak that protruded from the bottom of its tubular head and held something small and white to it. The cigarette flared as the squid took a drag.

"Took your bleedin' time didn't you buddy?" The other squid spoke in a clattering voice that put Steven in mind of the nightmares he used to have about ventriloquist's dummies. "Me and Basil was even thinkin' of leavin'."

"You guys are squids," Steven stammered.

"Well done that man. Regular Sherlock Blimmin' Holmes." The squid nudged his companion, Basil, with a tentacle. Strands of moisture hung between them. "Watch out Basil, he's on to you!"

"Eh?" Basil turned slightly to lean down over Steven. "But I ain't done nuffin'!"

"You're smoking," squealed Steven.

"What?" Basil lifted the cigarette in front of his eyes. His entire body turned a light shade of blue. With a whiplike motion he flung the butt away over the cars. "No, I never! Hang about." Basil turned to the other squid. "Gary, smoking's not illegal, is it?"

"I'm sure you weren't breaking any laws Basil. In fact, most laws don't apply to squid anyway, as written."

"You guys are squids," said Steven again, trying hard to emphasise that he was accepting the world that he was experiencing, but instead sounding like a frightened six year old confronted with the terrifying reality of the birthday clown they had demanded. This time both the squid leaned over him.

"Maybe he's had some sort of brain injury," said Basil in what Steven hoped was meant to be a whisper.

"You may be right," answered Gary. He moved from the roof of Steven's car down the windshield to the bonnet and then to the gravel of the car park. So, they hover, thought Steven as he watched the tentacles trail after Gary's body. The squid moved slowly towards him, lifting one paddle shaped "hand" to pat Steven gingerly on the shoulder. "Are. You. Oh. Kay?"

"Yes, I am." Steven stepped away from the paddle. "I'm just in a bit of shock. My clothes were very expensive and they've been ruined."

"How?"

"My girlfriend popped. And, on top of that, now there are flying talking squid on my car."

"Technically, we ain't flying," said Basil as he floated down from the car. "If I could fly then why do I pay so much to ride the buses!?" He hooted with laughter and his pupils looped around in circles. "Get it? Get it?" He jabbed Gary.

Steven was definitely less than an expert in squid biology but he was fairly sure that Gary gave the equivalent of an annoyed shoulder shrug before he answered.

"Yes Basil, I get it. You can't fly. Very good." His golden

irises focused on Steven. "I'm sorry about him. He doesn't get to come out here often and he's just had an ice-cream. That always amps him up."

"It had sprinkles."

"It did, indeed, have sprinkles, as you say. Now shut up."

Basil drifted back towards Steven's car, muttering all the way. "I don't see why you have to be so rude, I was just telling him about the ice-cream, you brought it up anyway, I didn't bring up ice-cream at all."

"Listen Steven," began Gary the Squid, draping a conspiratorial paddle over Steven's shoulders and dropping his voice. "It's just you and me here, right? No need for games. It's all been handled, do you follow me?"

"Where?"

"No ya dummy, I'm explaining things, you see?"

"See what? Do you mean it's all your fault? Why would you blow up Kate? She didn't even like squid rings, I always ended up eating hers."

"No, we didn't blow her up, that's my whole-" Gary's beak paused mid-sentence and his pupils did a quick loop. "I'm sorry. Did you just say that you ate squid rings?" His tentacle slipped off Steven's shoulders.

Basil sidled closer, which had the unfortunate effect of aligning his left eye directly with Steven's face like the headlight of a train.

"Uh." Steven glanced between the two squid, trying to figure out what to say. "Uh. Yes? Sometimes? If the Fish and Chip place does them on special?"

A gush of dark liquid squirted onto the gravel beneath Basil. "Oh oh oh; no, oh no, I'm so sorry, that hasn't happened to me in years, how embarrassing." He turned a faint blue again. Gary moved over to him and patted one of the triangular flukes that poked from either side of his head.

"No, that's okay mate, you got an awful shock there." He turned his gaze back to Steven. "I'm sorry your girl went pop mate, truly I am. But, squid rings? You should be ashamed of yourself."

Steven watched as the two squid began to move out of the car park. His mouth was hanging open and, after a minute, he realised this and closed it, before putting his hands in his pockets.

"Well, how do you like – Eurgh!" He pulled his hands out of his pockets again, strands of translucent ooze stretching between them. "What the – Hey! Hey Gary!"

The squid paused just beside a four wheel drive with the number plate MUMSBUS. It appeared to have one bag of groceries in the passenger seat and nothing at all in the other eight.

"What?" The squid's voice was faint with distance.

"I understand you guys weren't responsible, no matter what the waitresses say. But would you have any ideas how to get this gunk off my clothes? It's actually quite gross."

"I would have thought you'd want to treasure the last traces of your lovely lady?"

"Well yes, obviously that's the first thought I had, but the wind is carrying a bit of a chill with it and there's slime dripping from the back of my neck down my spine to my butt. This jacket was actually quite expensive too, so, y'know, dry and clean would be peachy keen."

Gary waved Basil on then came a short distance back towards Steven.

"You got no romance, you know that buddy?" The squid ran a paddle over its face, which was less effective as a sign of exasperation after one of his suckers got stuck and Gary had to spend a few seconds freeing it before continuing. "I'm not what you might call familiar with this particular neighbourhood. You'll have to find someone from around these parts to hook you up."

"But I don't know any laundromats or dry cleaners around here, what if they over charge me?"

"I really don't think that's my problem, is it? And now, if you'll excuse me." The squid saluted with one large flat paddle and then drifted back across the gravel towards Basil, who was waiting by the exit. Steven could see they began talking to each other as they moved off down the round. From the way they bobbed up and down, it seemed like they were laughing about something.

I don't see what's so funny about the situation, Steven thought. After all, this jacket was really quite-

"Psst, buddy."

Steven jumped at the sudden sibilant voice and spun to try and spot the speaker. The parking spaces around him were dotted with a variety of vehicles, but each one was clearly empty. No conspiratorial foreheads peaked over dashboards or from behind any car boots. Steven looked further, trying to determine if there was someone lingering by the large rubbish skips that were tucked into the greasy and blackened gaps behind the stores from the main road.

"No, over here man!"

This time the voice was definitely coming from behind Steven and he turned carefully to see. On the other side of the car park was a bright green painted metal fence that surrounded a small plastic playground in primary colours. A couple of mothers were pushing children on the swings or sitting together on the grass and talking. One of the kids had both hands tightly wrapped around the fence's bars and was staring at Steven.

"Come over here." The child, with its blonde curling hair tossing playfully about its pudgy face, crooked a finger at

Steven. He found himself walking over in a daze. It's all too much, he thought, I've probably just gone insane. Yes, that's it; I must have lost my mind.

"Glad you could make it," said the child. "My name's Bobby."

"Is that short for Robert?" asked Steven.

"What's that supposed to mean," scowled the child, hitching up its nappy as it did so. "You trying to figure out if I'm a boy?"

"Well," began Steven until he noticed another couple of children approaching the fence. They looked like someone had just stolen their lollipops and Steven realised he might benefit from carefully chosen words. He looked over Bobby's yellow t-shirt with a duck on it. "No, of course not," he finished.

"Good." Bobby nodded and waved the other children away. "If there's anything I hate, it's grown-ups who can't tell a boy from a girl, just because they're babies."

Steven smiled weakly.

"I understand you've been having a tough time today," said Bobby.

Steven nodded.

"Thought as much. When I saw you there talking to the squids, I figured you must be in some serious doody. They don't like to come out of the sea for anything trivial. Except ice-cream."

"Do you know what they wanted?"

"Not at all." Bobby shrugged. "But I do know that karma tends to help those who help someone who's gotten involved with those cephalopods. So, catch me up."

"I guess I may as well." Steven explained the situation to Bobby while the child stuck its thumb in its mouth and listened. There was a pause after Steven finished as the child continued to think, sucking softly on its thumb and fingering its earlobe.

"Are you sure that's all," Bobby finally said.

"What do you mean?"

"Had anything else happened before your girlfriend blew up?"

"I suppose you could say that. I had just asked her to move in with me actually. I thought it was time, and it would certainly have saved on expenses."

"What did she say to that?"

"Nothing. I was walking back to the table, we'd been discussing how she needed to leave her flat and I asked her to move in. Then she exploded and my jacket was almost certainly ruined. It cost me quite a lot."

"Well, then it's obvious isn't it?" The child shook its head at Steven. "She burst for joy."

Steven thought about it for a second. "I suppose that's possible," he allowed. "She did seem happy with me these days. But I don't think she wanted to ruin my jacket."

"That's even easier," said Bobby. "Did you pass Mulligan's on the main road?"

"Yes."

"That's my dad's dry-cleaners. I'll hook you up with a freebie."

And that's when Steven exploded.

I FOUND IT IN MY LETTERBOX

The houses on my street frowned at me. The windows to either side of their front doors dripped with rainy tears that made their lawns flooded and swampy. A cat floundered from the cover of some waterlogged trees towards its door, with mud-plastered fur. At first I thought it was a hedgehog gone wrong. The sight of the cat, struggling in circumstances that seemed designed to make it look its worst, reminded me of the twins. They both had the same short dark hair that was always sticking up in all directions, just like the cat's fur. And they were always in trouble too, just like the cat.

It was never their fault, of course. It was always the other kid who was teasing them, or the teacher who just didn't understand, or why had James bought so many bags of chips if he hadn't meant for them all to be eaten? They just took their punishment with a sullen glare and spent more time in their room with their phones, sending streaks on Snapchat. I couldn't blame them. Why should any of us bother explaining ourselves, when no one ever listens to us anyway?

Finally I reached my house. Before I went to the front door I stopped to get the mail. I knew it would be a pulpy mess of paper by now, but Dad would start yelling if there was anything in there when he got home. I pulled down the hatch of the letterbox.

It was sitting at the very back, behind a soggy mass of pulped bills and two slugs that were chewing at the already damaged letters. It was a very pale blue, the same sort of blue that the sky goes on a calm sunny day in winter, that faint colour that gives a reminder of summer between the black storm clouds that roll in from all sides. It was small too, about the size of a newborn kitten's paw, and just as fuzzy. It was difficult to tell where the edges of it were, or if actually the size was mostly light shining off something infinitely smaller. Thunder grumbled overhead, so I reached in and took it out.

Inside, I went to my room to get changed into something else, taking my soaking uniform and clothes to put them into the washing machine in the laundry straight away. I could feel it sitting in my pocket. It was warm, but the sort of warm that softly eased into your muscles like a balm, never burning anywhere. For the first time that day, I felt warm.

It had been cold that morning, and the olds had already been arguing when I woke up. A groan shuddered in my throat as I shook the grogginess from my head and drifted back into the real world. It was early on a black Friday morning. The sheet hung in a tangle off the side of the bed, leaving my right leg dangling off the edge of the mattress and my foot slowly freezing in the leftover night air. The chill crept up my leg and into my stomach. My parents' voices grumbled through the walls like distant thunder or crashing waves. Did they ever consider how thin the walls of our house were? Did they take a moment to think about the fact that me and the others could hear everything that happened in the lounge? The familiar thoughts flashed through my head and were gone, pointless questions.

"Then when will you be home?" My mother.

"I told you, I don't know, it depends how the work on the Toyata goes," came dad's standard response.

I rolled over and stuffed my head further into my pillow, grabbing the duvet and trying to pull it up around my shoulders. The pillow felt cool against my cheeks and ears. I pulled my foot in beneath the covers and rubbed it up and down against my other leg, hoping to build up a little heat that way at least. The darkness pressed in past my bedroom curtains.

"Oh come on, it's not like you've never worked on a car before. Make a guess."

"I can't. I told you, I don't know. Something could come up."

I shivered a little and sniffed, the cold air burning my nose.

"Something comes up every night. I don't understand how you find an emergency fault in a car every bloody day. Maybe, for once, you could let the damn car sit in the workshop until tomorrow and come home to be with your family?"

"It's not that simple, Diane. We service heaps of vans for the courier companies in Auckland, and they'll shift their business damn quick if we can't keep them running. If we don't stay late, Jaimee gets all sorts of crap from the clients on the phone. She needs my help." There was a rhythmic thudding as one of them stomped around the lounge. Probably my father gathering up his wallet and keys.

"I'm sure she does."

"What's that supposed to mean?"

"It means you've only ever introduced me to this Jaimee girl once, at the christmas party over a year ago, and you very quickly moved me away from her. What are you hiding?"

"What do you mean what am I hiding? What are you trying to say? Why would I be hiding something?" My father's voice was getting louder. The twins would be woken up by them soon.

"Well, you were certainly very uncomfortable with your wife talking to your pretty young receptionist!" My mother's voice was rising to match my father's. Great. I curled up a little tighter. There was a sliver of cold grey light at the top of my curtains, the colour of an iceberg.

"She's not really that pretty."

"Oh whatever, you're trying to avoid the subject. You didn't like her being reminded that you have a family at home."

"Maybe I just didn't think you two would have much in common to talk about? Jaimee's barely into her twenties and she cares about make-up and clothes and dressing up."

"And all I give a crap about is looking ugly?"

"I didn't say that!"

"You've always resented this family. You just wanted to be able to go out every night and play pool or drink beer with your mates. Flirting with skanky girls all across Auckland too, I'll bet. I'm sorry I ruined your pathetic little plan by having a baby."

"How dare you! I work myself to the bone, trying to keep you and these kids happy!"

"You haven't even been home all week! I think the last time you ate dinner with us was Monday."

"And what a feast you served up. Soggy broccoli and an overcooked lump of beef, smothered in barbeque sauce. Is it any wonder I find somewhere else to be in the evenings?" I tried pulling the duvet right over my head, but it couldn't keep out the cold.

"So you admit it! You admit that you are avoiding your own family."

"No, I'm not avoiding my family! But I'm certainly not in a rush to leave the shop at night. Somewhere where people appreciate the work I put in."

"You're finding excuses. You could be home by five thirty if you really wanted. Last night you got home at nine o'clock, the twins were already in bed!"

"They were in their room on their phones, sure. I'm certain that isn't doing their brains any favours, between the tiredness of being up so late and the mind-numbing videos they must be watching."

"Look, if you think you can do a better job with the kids, you get home in time for dinner! You put them to bed for a change!"

"We'll see." The front door slammed and the house held its breath.

I sighed and rolled my feet off the bed, rising to a slump on the edge of the mattress and shuffling my feet and shoulders in a desperate attempt to build up some body heat. Finally the noise had stopped. The light edging around curtains had barely brightened as my parents had argued.

I rummaged through my drawers for some clothes. My uniform wasn't there. I'd have to look in the laundry for the least smelly clothes. I sat, waiting until I heard the telltale slam that meant mum had left the lounge. Thank goodness, she would have retreated to her room, crawling back into bed until there was no way to avoid getting the twins to school. I wouldn't have to try and walk past her, to try and avoid the leftover anger twisting her face and making her snap at me for no reason. Only a few other signs to wait on now. Another door creaked in the hallway. Soft padding steps told me my older brother had made his way to the bathroom for his morning rituals. Perfect.

I slipped out of my room, closing the door carefully behind

me so that I wouldn't wake up the twins in their bunks behind me and have to deal with them. Far better to leave them asleep. I strode down the hall, ducking into the laundry and pulling yesterday's uniform off the pile. I sniffed at the cloth, coughing a little. I mean, it wasn't great, but it'd have to do. Then I moved through the lounge where the unwatched TV flickered and into the kitchen, where I found mum.

Crap, she hadn't gone back to her room. She was sitting at the small old table that we all usually ate at when there was nothing to watch on TV, despite the table's tiny size. She hadn't done her hair for the day yet, and black curls sprung out from a loose bun that swirled behind her head. Her dressing gown was made of thick fluffy material that should have been snug, but she'd had it ages and it was getting pretty tattered. It must be letting in draughts by now. She was holding a brown mug of tea between her hands on the table in front of her.

I coughed a little to clear my throat and then moved over to the cupboard and began to make myself a bowl of corn flakes. The toaster banged and shot two blackened pieces of bread into the air. Mum slowly made herself stand up and cross the room to the toast, pulling the slices onto two small plates and smearing each with a scoop of marge and then a whorl of marmite. She carried the plates back to the table, placing them next to her seat and then sat down again with her tea.

I sat down with my bowl of cornflakes and a spoon and looked at the chipped paint on the cupboards over the bench as I crunched my breakfast. The TV's murmuring came through the doorway, a morning talk show, discussing what little news they could scrounge from the night before. Occasionally the plastic hosts would laugh about something. I wondered if mum was even listening to them talk, or if she just liked having noise to drown out her thoughts.

"How's school?"

The question caught me by surprise and I choked a little on a flake. "What?"

"School. How's it going?" Mum wasn't looking at me as she spoke.

"Why?" I looked at mum for a minute. She didn't seem to be truly interested, just passing the time. She was already looking for something else in the room to occupy her attention.

"It's fine." I stuffed another spoonful of cornflakes into my mouth. Mum nodded. The wispy theme song of the morning show tinkled around us.

There was a clattering sound, like someone rolling a ball down a flight of wooden stairs. The sound rushed through the house and burst through the kitchen door along with the twins. My siblings were twins, a boy and girl named Libby and Jacob. But no one bothered remembering their names; they were always just 'the twins'. They swirled through the kitchen like a whirlwind, snatching up a plate each and then racing out of the kitchen just as quickly.

"A thank you wouldn't go amiss," growled mum, though she didn't bother moving to correct the kids. There was a click as they changed the channel of the TV in the lounge, followed by the shrieks and yells of whatever cartoon they were watching now. Without commenting, I spooned another mouthful of cornflakes into my mouth. The cereal squished softly between my teeth and mixed with the icy milk to create a sludgy mouthful of mush. How tasty. I swallowed with difficulty and then took a deep breath while I examined the stale bowl of cereal I had made myself.

"What's the matter with you?" asked mum, her hands still tight around her mug.

"Nothing." I finished my corn flakes and put the bowl back on the bench. I grabbed a brown-spotted banana from a small wire bowl on the bench, to take with me for some lunch. As I began to walk out of the kitchen, mum sighed and said "Tim, could you at least wash your bowl?"

"Aw geez mum," I rolled my head. "You know I need to get to school, you don't want me to be late do you? Mr Davies has been having fits about it recently." I kept walking into the lounge, blinking at the harsh light from the TV. The twins were watching some very geometric children bellow at each other about something.

"Turn that crap off, I can't hear."

The twins laughed "There's nothing to be listening to, ya egg!"

I got out of the lounge as soon as I could.

James must have finished getting ready, because the bathroom door hung open, wafts of steam drifting out into the hallway. One small cloud of moist air passed over me as I returned to my room, leaving my face clammy and damp. He appeared at his bedroom door just as I was about to close my own, gave me a barely perceptible nod and headed off down the hallway. I saw him poke his head through the lounge door to say goodbye, and then he swept out of the front door without hearing mum ask him to pick up some milk on his way home.

I grabbed my backpack from the foot of the bed and unzipped it, peering inside to check that I had all my books for the day. It looked alright, so I grabbed my camo beanie off the top of the drawers and headed off down the hall myself, following the same path James had taken. Mum had moved through to the lounge, standing behind the twins on the couch, looking out the front window. I wondered if she could still see James.

"And mum, you should be getting the twins dressed. It's already quarter to eight, don't be late yet again."

Mum groaned and turned to the twins. "Alright you two,

get out of here and get dressed, or I'm throwing you in the back of the car in your pajamas."

"Aw mum, there's only five minutes to go, can't we just finish the show?" one of the twins wheedled.

"No, get up!" Mum walked over to the TV and reached her hand down behind it. As usual, she was going to pull the plug out of the wall.

"Alright, alright!" The twins stood up and began to slink back towards the hallway. "This is so unfair, you are always so unfair, you never ever let us watch anything that we want to."

I closed the front door on the whines of the twins, glad to leave all that behind.

I WALKED into the house after school where I found Libby and Jacob were watching TV in the lounge so I sat down nearby. I watched the screen with them in silence for a minute or two. My find from the letterbox was tucked warm in my pocket. On the TV screen, some young man with a brightly coloured baseball cap was asking a young kid trivia questions and making the most ridiculous facial expressions as he did. He cracked out some unfunny jokes as he went, so bad that I almost had to smile. Next to me, Libby and Jacob didn't respond at all. I wondered why they had even turned it on.

"You guys got any homework?" I asked.

Libby looked at me. "Why?"

"Because it would be a good idea to do it now. Then you can watch TV without worrying about it."

"I'm not worried about it now." She turned back to the TV. My eyes narrowed and I felt the muscles in the back of my neck tighten. I opened my mouth to tell her off, but then just grumbled instead. There would be no point in trying to tell her off. That's what she was used to. The tiny globe of warmth in my pocket seemed to liquify and flow up my side and through my shoulder and neck, loosening the muscles like a masseuse. I sighed a little.

"What about you Jacob?"

He jumped in surprise. "Libby just told you," he answered, confused. His eyes darted back and forth between me and the television.

"I know, but she only said that she wasn't worried. Do you have anything that needs doing? Perhaps I could help."

Jacob pressed his lips together. "Really?"

"Yeah, if you like."

"Okay." He got up and walked slowly towards the hallway, watching me as closely as a mouse that has seen the cat hiding beneath the hedge nearby. I've never seen an eleven year old look more suspicious.

We moved through to the kitchen and set him up on the table there. I helped him with some maths equations for a while, though I found myself scratching my head over some of the word problems. I had never quite figured out how to tell which number needed to divide or be divided, so we ended up assigning two fifths of a muffin to five students, which was probably wrong. When we reached that answer, and I had frowned and picked up the question sheet to look closer, Jacob had even laughed. After we worked through a couple more, I left him to finish his worksheet. There was a bang as the back door slammed open and James came through, the wind and rain following him like a hungry dog howling for food. He shoved the door shut and stood staring at us, dripping water on the linoleum floor.

"What a waste," he muttered as he took in the worksheet covered in Jacob's writing. He wrenched the door of the fridge open and stared into the cold light inside.

"Hey man, you look freezing. Why don't you go have a hot shower and get changed."

"'What?" James blinked as he turned to look at me, clearly not taking in the words I had said.

"I just thought you might like to warm up." I slid my hand into my pocket, soaking up the warmth that was flowing from inside it. "Once you're in some dry clothes, we could make dinner for everyone."

"Mum always makes dinner." A single drop of water was sliding down James nose, almost to the tip. I reached out and flicked it off for him.

"We could do it tonight. Then dinner would be early, and she'd get something hot as soon as she got home."

The look on James' face was eerily identical to the look Jacob had given me. But he nodded slowly and squelched out of the kitchen towards the bathroom. Soon enough I heard a thud as the water started trying to pump through the old pipes in the house. I turned back to check on Jacob.

He was looking at me closely, with his pen poised a couple of centimetres above the worksheet.

"Are you okay?" I asked

"I was going to ask you that," he replied, before returning to the equations on the paper before him.

While Jacob kept working on his maths, I took out some vegetables and began chopping them into chunks, sweeping each one into a big pot of water that I started boiling on the stove. James joined me shortly, his hair still damp and the t-shirt he had pulled on sticking to him in places, but he defrosted some beef in the microwave and then began slicing it up and adding it to the pot too.

"Quick and easy," he said, smiling a little at me. "I'll get some stock in it, and maybe a bit of pasta if we've got some." I nodded and smiled back then finished cutting the last piece of carrot, put the chopping board in the sink and went back to the lounge to check on Libby.

Mum had arrived home while we were in the kitchen. Now I found her slouched into the couch in the lounge, staring at the flickering TV screen. The news was on, showing a pleasant looking man with a soothing voice calmly explaining that what they were about to show on the screen was distressing and some viewers may prefer not to watch. Mum didn't even blink. I went over to sit next to her.

"How was your day mum?" I asked.

She sighed. "It was fine, I suppose. Bill complained all day that I wasn't sending brochures to the right schools but he wouldn't tell me which schools to send them to. I ended up getting a list of every school from the Waikato to Whangerei and hoping that would be enough." Her shoulders slumped further. "It took a long time. But what else should I have expected?"

The lounge was cold and the light from the TV seemed harsh. It made the wrinkles in mum's cheeks and forehead stand out. I shivered a little.

"We got dinner started."

"That's nice. I suppose I'll have to make sure you don't burn anything." Mum pushed herself up from the soft cushions, groaning and rubbing the small of her back before heading towards the kitchen.

"No, mum, that's not what I meant!" I followed her.

James was stirring the pot of soup and watching Jacob working at the kitchen table. A rich smell seeped up from the pot and lazily trailed around the room. I had to swallow as my mouth started to water. Mum stopped.

"What's going on?"

"We thought we'd make dinner for you mum," said James with a smile. "We figured you'd probably be pretty exhausted."

Mum's forehead creased as she looked at her sons, quietly getting on with their chores. She scratched her wrist. "I don't get it."

"There's nothing to get mum," I said, coming up behind her and touching her shoulder. She jumped a little. "We just wanted to help out."

"Okay." She still seemed very confused. "I'll go have a lie down in my room then."

Jacob finished his homework and went into the lounge to watch TV. While he was packing up, I sat at the other side of the table and worked on my own assignments, making notes from a dog-eared Greek History textbook. I couldn't remember when I had last wanted to get my schoolwork done.

ONLY THAT MORNING I had been meandering and dawdling to avoid having to do any schoolwork as long as possible. But, even walking slowly, with my hands burrowed in my pockets and my chin hunched down to conserve what little warmth I could against the morning wind, I got to school with plenty of time to spare. I spent most of the 40 minute walk wishing I hadn't lost my school jumper earlier in the year, or that mum had sorted herself enough to buy me a new one already. While others sat with their friends, I leaned into a corner between two wings of the junior buildings and watched clouds scud across an icy blue sky, thickening and gathering. The wind was biting at my ears and cheeks this early in the morning and I scowled as I saw teachers emerge from their cozy staffrooms, cupping mugs of hot steaming tea or coffee between their fingers. The material of my pockets was thin, and I could feel the skin on my legs goose pimpling beneath it. I sniffed and blinked, then followed my first teacher of the day, Mrs Bell, as she wandered from the staffroom to her classroom. Maybe she would let me come into class early to warm up a little?

She wouldn't.

Morning break had crawled along eventually. I walked out under the grim grey sky and shivered. Two years in and I still hadn't found a good place to spend my breaks at this school. The tuckshop was surrounded by insanely cheerful and loud kids. Most of the courtyards between buildings were colonised by groups of handball-playing students, all of them far too involved in discussing the rules and strategies of one of the simplest games that has ever been devised for children. The green spaces and fields were filled with sports players and their fans. Even the smallest of patch of grass had a group of people passing a rugby ball back and forth. They spread out to fill the space more obviously as I walked by, carefully not looking at me.

I pulled out my banana as I walked. It had gained more bruises after a morning spent bouncing around my backpack, but it was all I had so I began to bite into the mushy flesh. A tennis ball smacked into the side of my face, jolting the banana out of my hand.

"Hey, sorry about that dude." Some little skinny junior came running over to retrieve his ball. "You alright?"

"No, you stupid little-" but he had already turned and started running back to his friends, waiting on their concrete squares. I gritted my teeth and clenched my hands tight, but there was nothing I could really do. Mr Sugawara was already trying to find reasons to get me in trouble, no matter how much I shut up in his classes. I looked at the squashed remains of my banana in the dirt by my feet. My stomach rumbled and I actually considered picking it up. Instead, I decided to go to the library.

The library was full of nerds, playing card games and

laughing, quietly so they wouldn't get kicked out. There was a group of people at the computers, playing some sort of simple shooter game. Apparently they had a club where they programmed games themselves. "Snobs," I muttered as I walked past them. Served them right, trying to be so poncy and proud of themselves, just for making a crappy game that no-one would ever have paid money for. One of them turned around and asked "What did you say?" but then the librarian scurried past and shushed them angrily. I shrugged and spread my hands wide as I smiled and walked away.

In the reading nook, full of worn out cushions, there was a corner that had oil heaters on both sides. It usually made a pretty good place to curl up and try to get warm. I shoved myself into the space, pulling my backpack around in front of me to be a sort of blanket or barrier. The heaters didn't feel very warm today, but there was a small flicker of heat left and so I pressed myself against the smooth metal and tried to soak in it as much as I could. Break only lasted another fifteen minutes, but I must have soaked up all the heat that remained, because the heaters were like blocks of ice by the time I trudged out to my next class. Clouds blotted out the sun.

The last lesson was agony, sitting inside on a Friday afternoon while some rare winter sun was beginning to strengthen outside the windows? I had to get out of here before my soul finally shrivelled up and died. Mr Young wouldn't stop talking and the clocked ticked slower and slower every time I looked at it.

"Excuse me sir," I said, lifting my hand wearily halfway in the air. "What is the point? I mean, Pompeii has some very nice buildings, but they all died. Every one, woman and children included, lovers and gladiators, rich and poor. There's no point."

The class giggled and Mr Young frowned. His neck began to

turn red. Maybe I should have kept my mouth shut. I was good at keeping my mouth shut, and I should have stuck to my strengths.

"It's important because we can learn about them Mr Williams," answered the teacher, pulling his glasses down his pale nose to look over them at me. "Their lives were frozen in a single moment and we can learn a great deal about what people of that time did for money and entertainment and-"

At that moment, just as my eyes were rolling in boredom, the bell rang. Thank goodness. I jumped to my feet, grabbed my bag and left the class. I was half jogging through the hall towards the doors that led outside, crossing my fingers that the sun would have warmed up, when there was a crack of thunder. The light dimmed.

"Oh come on," I muttered. A weight pulled at my stomach. Rain smashed against the glass doors and quiet shrieks of surprise echoed from outside.

Mr Young walked past me, pulling open a small black umbrella. "Well Tim, it looks like there was no rush to get out of my class after all." He smirked and stepped out into the rain, protected by his noxious little umbrella.

"Why am I surprised?" I asked myself. "I really shouldn't have expected anything else."

With every footstep closer to home, puddles sloshed over the tops of my shoes and soaked my socks, the cold water sinking into the softening skin of my feet. I had my hands buried in my pockets, but the school uniform was less a protection against the weather and more a water dispersal system, ensuring the icy liquid was deposited evenly across my body. I could feel my teeth beginning to chatter.

Getting out of my chair to leave had been so freeing. I had felt as though wings were growing from my shoulders, as though I were about to lift into the sky with the sun and swoop in joy to wherever I wanted. As thick wobbly drops of water trickled down the back of my neck, I realised that I hadn't escaped. I was going back to my dingy little house right now. I was just going to have to go back to school on Monday. I wasn't going to be going anywhere else, ever.

James had taught me that a long time ago really. He was three years older than me and he had always come home from school with stories about which teachers were the most boring, which ones gave the most tedious assignments. And he'd been right, as I found out when I managed to get a class with every single one of the teachers he'd mentioned. The same old boring work with no purpose.

My older brother had got an apprenticeship, to be an electrician or something. He said that at least there was money to be made there and maybe one day he'd be able to buy some time off. But every night he came home, his scraggly beard growing longer and yet at the same time somehow wispier, then collapsed on the couch and turned on the TV.

"Tim," he would groan, turning to me and ignoring Homer crack up as Moleman was hit in the groin with a football for the thousandth time. "It never gets better. They're always telling you what to think and what to do with your life. If it's not school, or your boss, it's your family. Mum keeps telling me to shave, or do my laundry. "You have to come to Grandad's Picnic"," he squealed in a mockery of mum's voice. ""Whatever would Grandma say if she noticed you weren't there?" It's all a waste of time."

"Yeah man," I would answer, pushing my homework to the other side of the lounge coffee table and staring at the TV. "There's no point."

"This show sucks," he would say.

. . .

After Jacob had finished his homework and gone into the lounge, while James was peeling some potatoes to add to the mix, as we didn't have any pasta, I came across a sub-heading on mythology in my textbook.

"Hey James, listen to this. "The story of Pandora helped to reinforce the position of women in Ancient Greek society. As a representative of all women, she was responsible for opening the box sent by Zeus and releasing all of mankind's woes into the world. Though there are variations on the ending, traditionally Hope is a small frail creature that is subsequently released from the box. It is the presence of Hope in the world that allows humanity to withstand the trials it faces." What do you think of that?"

"Sounds very hokey to me," said James, though his mouth curled up towards a smile at one side as he said it.

"I think it sounds kind of... nice."

I thought of the small blue thing that was still safely tucked into my pocket, then pulled it out and placed it on the table in front of me. It bobbed up and down against the surface of the table, washing my hands in its pale colour. James came over and took the seat Jacob had been sitting in.

"Wow," he breathed. "What is that?"

"I don't know. It was in the letterbox."

Neither of us could think of much else to say and so James asked me to keep an eye on the soup in case it boiled over while he went to catch up on some study for an assessment he had to do with his apprenticeship. An hour passed, in quiet. I could hear the scratch of my pen on paper, the rustle of the rain pattering on the roof, a quiet laughter from the TV in the lounge and the hissing and popping of the soup. I felt that safely-wrapped-up feeling that comes as you fall closer and closer to sleep, though I was completely alert.

Soon enough I heard James' voice from the other end of the house.

"Come on everyone, that soup should be ready by now. Dinner's on!" There was a muffled thump of doors swinging open and closed, and the TV was switched off. I took the blue object from its spot next to my books and slipped it back into my pocket. My stomach felt like it was being squeezed softly, so I was glad the stew was ready. Jacob's bare feet made slapping noises on the kitchen floor. "This smells great! Thanks James."

"You're welcome," answered our older brother. He came into the room with Libby close behind. Her eyes were dark and she was frowning.

"Why couldn't I just eat in my room," she grumbled.

"Because we're being a little bit more civilised today," said James.

Mum slipped into the kitchen as we scooped ladles of thick meaty soup and chunks of vegetables into our bowls. She glanced around and made a clicking sound with her tongue.

"Where's your father?"

I couldn't help but flinch. I knew from the argument in the morning that it was pretty unlikely that he was going to be home at any reasonable hour tonight, but so did mum. I checked the time on the microwave. The green flashing numbers said it was about six.

"I'm sure he's fine," I said. The warmth of the soup from the bowl in my hands was seeping along my arms and down my chest. It mixed with the warmth coming from my pocket and made me smile. I felt like the thing in my pocket was going to float out and hover in the air between us.

"No, after this morning, he should know better. He knew he needed to be home on time tonight." Mum took the opportunity to pull out her cellphone and swipe the display. "Nope, definitely no missed calls or texts. He's avoiding me."

"What do you mean, "avoiding you"? Mum, you don't know that he's doing anything deliberate."

"Yes I do," mum scowled. "He's trying to teach me a lesson. It won't work. He's the one who should have changed his behaviour after all that crap!"

For a moment the room seemed smaller, darker and colder.

But as we slurped at our food, we all began to sit a little straighter. Mum asked how the twin's day had gone at school, and Jacob told her about a game he had invented with his friends during lunch. It involved a lot of running and climbing trees, and I wasn't sure what the point of it was, but he said that his friend Tyler had won and that seemed to please him, so we all congratulated him on his creativity. Libby mumbled something about having to do some boring writing.

"What sort of writing was it," I asked.

"Just writing. It was boring." She slurped at a spoonful of her soup.

"I'd like to hear about it." James said. He and mum both turned to watch Libby. Her neck flushed a little and she looked down deeply into her bowl before answering.

"It was just a story thing. We had to write about a child in another place."

"What place did you write about?" asked James.

"I wrote a sort of a fairy tale. About a girl who grew up and defeated a dragon by tricking it into drinking a river."

"That sounds pretty cool," said mum.

"Yeah, I guess it was kinda cool," Libby said, smiling a little.

"Could you bring it home? I'd like to read that," I asked.

"Okay!"

Libby finished the last of her dinner and leaned back in her chair, with her head high. The air in the kitchen was still warm from the stove and all our bellies were full. Then mum took out her cellphone and frowned at the small glowing screen. She sighed through her nostrils and punched the screen heavily with her fingertip. I grimaced, almost expecting the screen to crack beneath the pressure.

"What are you doing mum?" I asked.

"What do you think," she grumbled. "I'm trying to call your father."

"I'm sure everything's okay-" I began but she just shook her head and held her phone to her ear. Libby began to slouch down in her chair and Jacob started tapping his empty bowl with his spoon. The sound hung in the air, ringing sharply in our ears.

"Would you stop that?" snapped mum. James got up and carried the empty bowls to the sink, running the tap so that they began to soak. The rain battered against the roof outside, rattling on the windows. It was pretty dark by now, with only a cold grey light coming in from outside. No one had thought to put on the lights in the kitchen, so we were sitting in deepening shadow.

"Dammit!" Mum gripped the phone in both fists and squeezed her eyes shut. "No answer."

"Can I help you with those?" I tried to ask James, but he just shook his head and left the kitchen. The twins slunk after him. I moved over by the door and turned on the light. Mum sat alone at the table, with a dull orange filament the only light above her. It left her eyes looking like long dark shadows and made her skin seem lighter. My stomach was beginning to feel cold again. I clutched at the object in my pocket, but it didn't seem as warm anymore.

"I'll try the workshop," said mum, with a weary resignation in her voice. I watched as she spoke briefly to someone on the other end of the line. "Thank you for that." She hung up and looked at the empty wall beside her, not meeting my eyes. "He left an hour or two ago. Most of the staff did."

An unspoken name hung in the air. I wanted to ask who she had spoken to. I wanted to say something to my mother. To make her realise that things would be okay. That at least I loved her and wanted to help. But my tongue was frozen in my mouth and I couldn't think of anything to say.

"I knew he was upset, but I never thought..." Her voice trailed off. The icy feeling in my stomach stabbed up into my ribs and pricked my heart. I left the kitchen.

I walked through the darkness of the house, not sure what I was looking for. The twins sat in the unlit lounge watching a cartoon that seemed to involve a small rodent causing severe pain to a seemingly timid cat. Shrieks and yells burst out of the speakers and burrowed into my head.

"Could you turn that down?" I snapped at the twins. They didn't even look up to acknowledge my words. I kept walking, into the hallway.

Just as I walked past the front door, there was a banging on it. I rushed over and flung it open, hoping to see my father standing on the doorstep. As I did so, I realised that he would have had a key. And that the door was unlocked.

Standing on the step, drenched from head to toe, stood the surliest delivery man I have ever seen in my life. Water dripped from his eyebrows and he blinked continuously in an attempt to be able to see. His pale skin looked unctuous and fish-like in the damp glow of the streetlights.

"Don't suppose you're Diane then?" he said.

"Uh," I began, but he didn't wait to hear me.

"There a Diane live here?"

"Mum?" I yelped. She appeared behind me in the hallway before long.

"Yes?"

"Delivery for you?"

The delivery man held out a bouquet. It had held up surprisingly well, considering the wind and rain outside. Though it was ruffled, the flowers were still bright. The drops of water on the petals and leaves looked like tiny diamonds. The man held out a small electronic tablet.

"Need you to sign for 'em thanks." he grumbled, shrugging his sodden jacket up his shoulders to try and cover more of his neck. Mum took the bouquet and tucked them under one arm as she signed the tablet. The man gave a sharp nod and turned to sprint back to his van.

"Good of him to work so late," I said. Mum snorted and headed back to the lounge. I followed.

"Are they from dad?" I asked.

"Probably," said mum.

"That's nice," I ventured.

"It would be," she agreed. "If it meant anything. If he thinks this is enough to mollify me after this morning, especially when he has kept us waiting so late." She shook her head. "I bet this is just his conscience trying to pay me off. He knew what was going to happen and... " She paused. I couldn't see her face but the next breath she drew was long and ragged. "He's done something else and now he feels guilty. Typical of him, make matters worse and then just thrust some flowers at me to ignore the real issues. At least he usually does it in person, this is just insulting." She dropped the bouquet onto the display cabinet that held photos of all the family, our aunts and uncles, cousins, grandparents, all watching over us . Then she returned to the kitchen. I looked at the twins. They were staring at the mad-eyed cartoon on the TV screen.

I had never realised just how dark our house could get. The storm still beat down outside, and the wind howled infrequently. I walked down the hall and knocked on the door to James' room.

"What?"

"Can I come in?"

"Why?" James's voice was muffled and distant, though I knew he could only be sitting a metre or two beyond the closed door.

"Just to talk."

"I'm busy."

"I just feel kind of alone."

I waited for a count of one hundred, hoping that my brother would reply to me. But he didn't. So I turned away from the closed door and went into my own room and lay down on top of the blankets on my bed. I listened to the wind and rain outside and felt the cold and dampness begin to leak into my thoughts. My head felt cold, and the feeling trickled down the back of my neck and across my chest. Something had changed today. Things had been the way they always were, lifeless, but then they had become vibrant. Something had been good, but I couldn't explain why it had become good, and now it had gone away again. Now I was left in the dark, but with knowledge of the warmth I had felt. I missed it. I kept one hand in my pocket, squeezing as carefully as I could to try and find it again.

I don't know how long I lay in the dark, but I must have begun to fall asleep because a loud bang shook me awake. There were loud footsteps coming from the front door, and another thud as the front door was slammed shut.

"Diane?!" came the voice of my father.

"Good of you to finally join us!" yelled my mother in reply from some other room. I swung my feet off the bed and sat on the edge, listening to the argument escalate.

"... at least have called to say where you were!"

"Look, I work very hard to provide for you all, and where is the gratitude?"

"Oh, and I don't? What sort of..."

Their voices mixed together into a jabbing aharmonic chorus of anger. I stood up and moved to the hallway. It felt as though the storm had come inside, and the wind was trying to push me away, back down the hall.

"...are you saying? Are you accusing me of something?"

"What could I possibly accuse you of? Have you done anything you should feel guilty about?"

"Don't you dance around the issue Diane, if you've got something to say you just spit it..."

Their tempers cracked and stabbed like icicles in my ears, icy crystals catching in the corners of my eyes. The object in my pocket felt cold now, as small and smooth as a marble. Behind me I heard the door to James' bedroom creak as it opened. I reached the end of the hallway and opened the door to the lounge.

Mum and Dad were standing at opposite sides of the room, flailing their arms in the air as they yelled at each other. The twins had shrunk down as low as they could into the cushions of the couch, caught in between our warring parents. Dad had managed to remove his work jacket and fling it onto one of the chairs in the corner of the room. Mum had soap on her arms. I supposed she must have begun cleaning the dishes. I wished I had done them for her, instead of going to my room. The object in my pocket felt a little warmer.

"Could you have blamed me staying away? What are we eating tonight, more barbeque sauce meat? KFC would be more filling and I'd actually enjoy eating for a change!"

Mum snatched up a coaster from the coffee table and flung it at dad.

It was an impulsive throw, so it tumbled through the air

like a sick bird instead of spinning like a discus, but it moved fast enough that dad had to duck to avoid it cracking into his face. The smack of the wooden coaster hitting the wall behind him sounded as sharp as an axe splitting wood. It ricocheted into the shelves of photos, knocking a photo of our family from two christmases ago to the floor. The glass in the frame shattered with a crack.

"What the hell is wrong with you woman?" bellowed my father. The storm outside boomed with thunder that rolled and echoed back and forth through the room, only quieting as my own heartbeat settled. The twins slipped lower and lower off the couch, looking as though they wanted to crawl away across the floor like frightened cats.

James stepped up next to me and shut the door to the hallway behind him. The noise didn't seem to distract mum or dad, whose eyes were locked on each other, glaring out from faces twisted in anger.

"We actually have some lovely dinner tonight, David." Mum's voice hissed out from between her teeth. "Soup, made by your own sons. Would you like to insult their cooking now David?" She waved a hand in our direction.

"What?" Dad seemed confused. "No, of course I'm not going to insult the boys."

"Oh, so it's only me you want to insult is it?" The question hung temptingly in the cold air. Rain drummed on the roof. "It's only me, your wife, who you swore to love, that you can't stand to be around, huh? It's only your ugly wife who isn't as appealing as the young receptionist at your work?"

I felt like my heart was turning to rock. My neck was tight and the muscles in my jaw were tense. I wanted to yell at them both for being selfish, for creating a monstrous presence in our lounge, for letting their bickering overflow and explode in front of us. I wanted to scream at dad for being late again, for insulting my mother again, for not caring about how we got through our days. I wanted to shout at mum for making threats but never following through, for taking the worst interpretations of everything we said, not just what dad said. I wanted to grab James and tell him to just grow up and get on with making the best of what he has, instead of languishing as though his life was only made of pain. I wanted to bellow at Libby and Jacob for never trying to help, for never considering how they could add something good to our family. I clenched my fists and squared my shoulders.

"- even that late! What do you have a problem with this time?" Dad was saying.

"Could you two think about what you are doing right now?" I realised it was my voice that had cut through the argument.

Their eyes turned to me.

"I mean, all your children are right here. We couldn't even avoid this if we wanted to!" I could hear that my voice was about to break.

"This has nothing to do with you Tim!" Mum was still loud, but her voice was lowering. "This is on your bloody father."

"Oh, I'm his bloody father now am I? That's nice. Why don't you watch your language in front of the kids? Isn't that like you, to do something irresponsible yourself and then say it's my fault, that you're only reacting to what terrible things I have done!"

Mum turned back, and I could see that the fight would only continue. I hadn't even distracted them. I put one hard into my pocket and felt the small round ball tucked deep at the bottom. The cold in my stomach was sharper than a knife now, it nearly made me vomit. There had to be something new.

"I'm just glad that he's home."

Mum turned back to me now. My hand felt ever so slightly warmed.

"I just wanted us all to enjoy a hot meal. To sit together and talk."

Now dad was looking at me too. I felt James put a hand on my shoulder.

"I had a good day today. The boss said I was doing really well with the wiring of this house we're working on."

Our parents looked at each other.

"I wrote a story," said Libby from the floor between them.

"I invented a new game with Tyler," said Jacob, slowly moving up to stand from his crouch.

Mum looked at her feet. Warmth spread along my arm slowly, as though I was holding a mug of milo.

"Mum was worried that something had happened to you," I told dad. "But I'm sure you knew that. Couldn't you just tell her why you are late?" I walked over to him and gave him a small hug around his shoulder. "I am glad you're home."

Dad looked around the lounge. His mouth opened and closed a few times. He made eye contact with mum for a long time before looking back at me.

"I didn't mean to make you worry." He leaned over and gave me a quick hug as well. My stomach began to settle. "The storm blew over phone wires and flooded streets. It's been hell trying to get back here."

"Yes, you said." Mum's voice sounded unimpressed, though she didn't shout this time. "And what were those flowers for? To apologise for your bull-headedness this morn-ing? Because if you think that I'll-" Her voice began to rise but dad raised his hands in submission.

"No, I'm sorry about this morning. I sent those flowers because I was thinking today how lucky I am to have this family. Didn't you read the note?"

"What note?"

Libby got up out of the couch and picked up the bouquet where it lay on its side on the side cabinet. "There's no note dad," she said, turning to show him.

"That's strange, I know I ordered one."

"Wait a minute," said Jacob, as he bounded to his feet and zipped out of the room. There was a clatter at the front door and then he returned with a small wet white piece of card, drooping in his hands. "It was stuck in the rosemary by the front door. The delivery guy must have dropped it."

He walked over to mum and handed it to her. She read it quickly and then looked up at my father. ""Just for being you. I'm lucky to have you all. I look forward to dinner with you all tonight." That's sweet Michael, it is."

"Good, I'm glad you like it." He nodded and turned to the rest of us. "I didn't mean to yell in front of you two," he said, walking over to crouch down in front of Libby and Jacob. He picked up the remote and muted the TV. "I'm sorry I was yelling at your mum in front of you. I shouldn't have done that." He hugged the two of them together. James came into the lounge and turned on the light. The room seemed so much bigger and more open after that. Mum came over and hugged Dad too, though from the hurried whispers that they exchanged I figured there was going to be a long conversation once they were alone. The warmth was spreading further, loosening my muscles.

Dad enjoyed his soup very much, and told Jacob he thought the game sounded a lot like something he had played with his friends when he was younger. He finished his dinner and washed up the bowl, listening to Libby explain the story she had written at school. Then he made two cups of tea, adding a small spoon of sugar to his own and asked James and I to leave him and mum alone so they could chat in the lounge.

I hugged them both good night, enjoying the warmth that spread through my shoulders as I did.

"Are you okay?" I asked mum quietly as I hugged her.

"I am," she replied. "I just got a little scared. Thank you for being so positive today."

"That's okay."

While I waited for James to finish brushing his teeth, I stood in the hallway. The buzz of his electric toothbrush hummed through the door and bounced around the hall, but I found that I could hear the low murmur of mum and dad talking in the lounge, like the crackle of a fire. If I strained my ears I could even catch the occasional phrase, like "but then" or "you see" but then they would laugh softly and I decided that I didn't need to listen to any more. There was a pale glow from underneath the door to room Libby, Jacob and I shared, a ray of sunlight from between the rain clouds. The light shifted and flickered as they played some sort of game on their phones. I moved to the door, about to knock and tell them it was late and they should go to sleep. As I did, the light flicked off. I shook my head and smiled to myself.

The carpet in the hall felt familiar as I paced along it in the darkness. James would be nearly done, and then I could do my own teeth and get to sleep. I felt tired, but in the way that an athlete or construction worker might do after a big task. I felt as though I had worked for my tiredness, and sleep would be a fair reward. The front door made a slight thump as it was shifted by the wind outside. I walked closer and gently opened it.

Outside the storm was still raging. The night was thick with darkness and the wind was shoving at me, trying to shoulder its way into the house, bringing its cold and it's damp into our sanctuary. I stepped through the door and swung it shut behind me. The automatic light came on, casting its meagre beam around me on the front step, leaving me feeling very alone.

I reached into my pocket and pulled out the blue object. It was warm, though not nearly as warm as it had been when I found it. Then it had been a hot water bottle in my pocket, now it was a cup of Milo that had been left to cool down. Its light was so delicate, like the petal of a flower that had been dipped in liquid nitrogen. I felt as though just breathing wrong would crush it forever. It sat, trembling, cupped in my hands to protect it from the buffeting winds. The rain soaked through my flannel pajamas within moments.

I looked down the street, at the houses of all the people who lived around me. I could see at least one light in each house, trapped behind curtains and doors. I wondered what sort of day all the people in those houses might have had. The rain began to trickle down my collar again, carrying a chill to my spine.

I held it out, and opened my fingers. The wind caught it and carried it away into the night. The storm howled.

I stood for some time in the storm, feeling the cold bite at my fingertips and the water seep into my skin. But try as it might, the storm never touched me deep inside. My stomach felt settled and warm. With a smile I went back inside to my family.

PERSPECTIVE

So I held my breath until I turned blue,
wailed from my cot
and soaking my swaddling cloths in tears
then hurled soft toys onto the floor.

I heard my voice echo back
from walls muralled with horizons
and only the brightest colours could be found there.

Each grain of sand, each pebble,
only served to fill my lungs.

And then you walked in
With a mountain on your back,
and shattered the walls of my room.
You lifted me and held me,
you soothed my brow.
You cleaned the wreckage from the floor,
bent double.

And from the heights you carried with you,
beyond the broken walls I saw,
in greasy, dirty detail,

The Real World.

OMENS

"They're bad luck."

Tom looked up from the newspaper he had spread across the counter next to the cash register. Matt was clutching a cardboard box full of plastic soft drink bottles, on his way to a small drinks fridge.

"Energy drinks are unhealthy man, not bad luck."

"No! Those birds." Matt tried to point with his chin but nearly dropped the box. "Over there."

Tom looked in the direction of the shop's door, which was wedged open by an old tattered sneaker that Matt had found next to the rubbish skip behind the store. A flutter of movement caught his eye. It was a fantail.

The little round bird hopped from the newspaper stand to the edge of a shelf of chocolate bars and then to the floor, tilting its head to allow the gold black sphere of its eye to take in the surroundings.

"It's just a fantail Matt," shrugged Tom.

"Yeah, it's a just little bird, but it's still bad luck dude."

The bird appeared to be puffing up its wispy grey chest feathers. Occasionally it spread its tail feathers, which were so long they doubled its length.

"It looks kind of pretty man. Like a sort of fancy sparrow."

Matt pursed his lips as he put his box of drinks on the floor beside the fridge. He looked from Tom to the bird and back. He raised his eyebrows. "I'll just shoo the bird out of the store shall I?"

"That'd be great, thanks man." Tom looked back at the newspaper. Matt made a growling sound and walked over to the door, waving his arms.

"Shoo! Shoo! Get out of it, you diseased powder-puff!"

"Hey, steady on, there's no need to get personal," said Tom as the bird flew up to perch on the fluorescent light that hung above the counter. The two young men crossed their arms and looked at the bird.

"So, why are they bad luck?"

"They're a symbol. Like a black cat crossing your path, a fantail in the house is a sign that death will be coming. Hey!" He jabbed a forefinger at Tom. "We could lure it out instead!"

"How? It looks pretty comfy up there man." Tom leaned against the cupboards behind him. "He's not hurting anyone." The fantail tilted its button eye towards him.

"Not now, but what if it starts pecking open the chips or something? Those things carry as much disease as rats or mice. We can't leave it here."

"Maybe it'll only eat the bugs and spiders and stuff? That'd be useful; we could let it stay then."

Matt shook his head as he walked over to a shelf full of potato chip packets. He took a small shiny foil packet and tore open the top before answering Tom. "You're too soft-hearted Tom. Sometimes you have to be cruel to be kind." He began breaking off small pieces of the chips and throwing them on the ground near the door.

"You're feeding him. Is that being cruel to be kind?"

Matt just rolled his eyes and backed out the door, dropping more pieces of chips.

After a moment the fantail flew down from the light and peered at the food. It bounced in a circle around the food, looking sideways. Then it pecked at the chips, though it didn't seem to eat any, and then headed out the door, looking for something else.

"See ya bud," said Tom. He smoothed out a crease in the newspaper and continued reading.

He had barely had time to find out about the injury that had sent a local rugby player to the bench during last weekend's game when he heard voices.

They were young and chirpy, like a nest of chicks excited over the delivery of worms. Tom hung his head.

Five kids sauntered into the store, pushing one another's shoulders and talking without listening to each other. Tom felt the muscles across his shoulders grow tense as he watched them fingering everything in the store, leaving greasy marks on the fridge doors and creasing the covers of the women's gossip magazines.

"Can I help you guys?' he called as they disappeared behind some shelves. The response was just giggling.

Matt stepped in the door and wandered over to speak to Tom at the counter. "Well, I tried to get it to go to the park or something but it just keeps flying back to our roof. At least it's not inside anymore."

"Unfortunately, they are though." Tom walked out from behind the counter to point out the ten-year-old boys crouched by the biscuits.

"Oh fantastic."

Matt and Tom walked together towards the boys. When the boys finally noticed them approaching, they stood up and one with a shaggy head of bleached hair stuck his hands behind his back and grinned.

"Alright dude, what have you got," sighed Tom.

"What do you mean? I ain't got nothin'." The other boys snickered. Matt frowned and shoved his hands onto his hips.

"Behind your back. You're clearly holding something. What is it?" asked Tom.

"Oh, this?" The boy brought forward a snack sized packet of crackers.

"I was going to buy these for lunch." His smile glistened up at Tom. "Do you have a problem with that?"

"You were going to buy them huh?" Tom was about to tell the kid how easy it was to spot a lying ten year old when one of the others piped in.

"Yeah, course he was. You trying to say otherwise?" This boy wore a t-shirt that would have been too big on Tom. He didn't smile like his friend, his nostrils flared and the whites of his eyes nearly glowed.

"You guys are planning to cause trouble," said Matt. "I want you to leave."

"C'mon guys," said baggy t-shirt. "We don't want to shop somewhere that we get told off, even though we haven't done anything, do we?" The others shook their heads.

Blondie threw his crackers on the floor and looked up at Tom. "I changed my mind."

Tom picked up the packet and put it with its fellows on the shelf, while Matt followed the kids to the door. They walked as slowly as they could without Matt pushing them along. Some even stopped to look closer at a pack of batteries or tissues. Tom pinched the bridge of his nose as they finally walked out the door. He began to walk back to the counter.

"Those little bastards!"

Tom rushed to the window. "What did they do?"

"Just look."

The boys were running across the open grass of the reserve next to the store. Tom could see them throwing things to each other.

"What are they throwing?" he asked.

"Cookies," muttered Matt. "I don't know how they hid them, but they did. They stole about three bags of cookies."

The boys were hard to see clearly now, but Tom could tell they were heading to the walkway on the other side of the reserve, a footpath between two houses that lead to another street beyond.

"There's no way we'll catch them, is there?"

"Not now. But hopefully they'll be dumb enough to come back." Matt rubbed his hands together. "I'll never forget those arrogant little faces, and you just wait till I get my hands around their scrawny little necks." He ran a hand over his face, snorted and headed back to where his cardboard box still sat next to the fridge.

While Matt began putting drinks away Tom watched the boys vanish down the footpath. He thought he saw a speck of grey shoot from the roof to the trees in the park, but it was too small and fast to be sure.

The rest of Tom's shift passed quietly. There were only a few customers so he and Matt spent most of their time laughing about recent episodes of their favourite TV shows. The blue sky was beginning to darken and a cool breeze beginning to rise when Tom waved to Matt and started the walk home. He crossed the reserve with his hands pushed deep in his pockets, then entered the walkway.

A small girl stood in the middle of the path in front of Tom. She had black hair that hung in a straight curtain to her shoulders. Her eyes were closed and she held her hands together in front of her chest. Tom wondered if she was ill, as she wore only a plain grey dress and bare feet which didn't look comfortable as night drew in with a chill in the air. Yet she didn't shiver.

"Excuse me?" Tom reached out to touch the girl and changed his mind. "Are you okay? Are you lost?"

The girl opened her eyes and Tom felt his heart lurch towards his throat. She tilted her head to the right and looked at him with black eyes like inky marbles.

"Do... Do you need some help?"

The girl smiled, her lips shifting only slightly. "There's no need to get personal," she said. Her voice tinkled like the patter of water over stones in a tiny creek.

"I wasn't, I mean; I didn't... Did I?" Tom felt his cheeks grow warm.

The girl moved to the side of the path and waved Tom on with her left hand. Her smile remained in place, like a porcelain doll's. "See ya bud."

Tom edged around the girl, unwilling to turn his back to her. He felt like the deep black of her eyes was going to swallow his. He moved backwards down the path, sliding his feet through small clumps of fallen leaves to avoid stumbling. Soon he rounded a corner and left the girl behind.

What on earth was all that about? Tom thought. The skin on the back of his neck felt like someone else's, loose and warm.

The dark was closing in above him as he walked further down the path. Shortly he approached the other end of the footpath, positioned between two letterboxes. A hedge replaced the corrugated iron fence on his left and a large flowering bush to his right. Beneath the flowers was a green t-shirt in a crumpled pile.

Tom stopped to examine the clothes. There was something wrapped inside. Dark stains soaked the material like damp maps of dangerous lands. Tom leaned down.

He lifted the t-shirt slowly. The contents clattered to the dirt below. Tom felt his throat clench and he gagged. The bones on the ground still had chunks of red flesh stuck to them. A jawbone lay on top of the pile, silver fillings visible even under the dimming sky.

Tom was shivering in his jacket. Breathing heavily, he turned and began to trudge back down the path.

The girl was standing with her back to him. The sight was twisted, her body seemed to retreat inside her outline, curving away from him as though he was looking at the inside of a balloon. Tom swallowed. His throat was still tight but he didn't feel like throwing up anymore. He could feel a drop of cold sweat running down his spine.

"Did you do that? What did you do?" Tom heard his voice cracking.

The girl turned and blinked her coal-black eyes. Her cheeks creased.

"Shoo! Shoo! They're bad luck." She held her hands in front of her lap.

"The... the kids? Are bad luck?"

The girl didn't move.

"Did you kill them?"

"Sometimes you have to be cruel to be kind."

"Oh god." Tom squeezed the bridge of his nose. "What are you?"

The girl tilted her head and shimmered, like a reflection in a pond, disturbed by the wind. On the path, in her place, a tiny fantail hopped from leg to leg.

Tom chewed his lower lip.

"I only saw one t-shirt," he muttered.

The fantail fluttered up to a branch near his head, spread its tail and flew off over the houses.

Tom watched it go and then closed his eyes. His hands were still shaking. Finally he began walking back towards the store.

"Maybe Matt won't think they're bad luck anymore..."

I SEE YOU

She sits with her friends
at the other end of the picnic table.
Cigarette smoke hangs in the air between us.
Speakers shake the car parked nearby,
my friends shout and laugh over the music.

Our eyes meet.

One by one the others go to sleep.
Empty beer bottles piled among bent bottlecaps.
The sky is clear, the breeze is cold
and in the middle of the night we sit closer
talking about nothing.

Our eyes meet.

THE UNSETTLING CASE OF YOUNG JOSEPH PRICE

Officer Jacob Anderson sat in *The Wounded Hound*, his favoured pub, with his old friend John Wallace. The Officer sat still and quiet, eyes low. He sipped slowly at his glass of beer.

"Is something the matter Jacob?" John asked finally, seeking to comfort his friend who was clearly feeling brought low.

The policeman shook himself and sighed. "I've taken some details about a young man in the last few days, and the situation leaves me with an odd feeling at the back of my head. I feel as though I have been granted a glimpse of something awful that is hidden all around us."

"What happened?"

CORA ROBINSON'S INITIAL STATEMENT

Thank you for helping me sir.

Earlier today, a message had come that my good friend Mister Joseph Price would be delighted to accompany me to the roller skating rink in the evening and I had been in good spirits as I prepared for the outing. I had made the acquaintance of Joseph early last summer and now we had reached a stage in our courting that I referred to with my mother as 'An Understanding'. I was beginning to wonder whether this Understanding would soon progress into a more official state of affairs, but for now I was enjoying our regular get-togethers.

"Good afternoon Miss Robinson," he said with a twinkle in his eye when he arrived to walk with me.

"Good afternoon to you sir," I replied. "Has your day treated you well since I saw you last?"

"Indeed it has," he exclaimed. "My studies continue apace, and I am managing to complete my assignments in good time and to pleasing results."

"You have complained that the doctor seemed distracted of late, causing interruption to your studies. Has that changed?"

"Unfortunately not," sighed my companion. We turned in on the path, closer to the houses, as another couple walked past in the opposite direction. A carriage trundled along the cobbles. "He has been as knowledgeable as ever in his lectures, but his voice is lower in each subsequent speech, and it has become nearly impossible to understand him beyond the first rows. He mutters now most often about some salt, and how to remove impurities from our samples. I fear the esteemed Doctor Jekyl may be losing his grip on the subject." Joseph frowned momentarily, but then his attention flicked back down to me and he smiled. He lifted a hand to pat the back of mine. "This is part of why I am especially grateful to spend the afternoon walking with you Miss Robinson."

I smiled again, and felt a small shiver of pleasure along my shoulders. I put my arm in his and we continued our walk to the rink.

The skating rink is a popular destination for other young couples as well, and we found the line waiting to enter close and hot. It was difficult to speak, for while one could be fairly sure that the jostle and hubbub of the crowd would render it nigh impossible to eavesdrop, the same sounds and difficulties made hurdles for one to hear one's companion also. After a few attempts at conversation in the queue, Joseph and I contented ourselves with the occasional meeting of one another's eyes and smiling. I felt a flush of happy warmth with my fingers resting upon his arm. Then, we were inside.

The rink was full of laughing men and women, all spinning around in a long lazy circle on their roller skates, some holding hands or with linked arms. A group of six or seven was rushing around the rink in a line, threatening to bowl over slower skaters who were unable to get out of their way in a hurry. I covered my mouth as I watched them pass.

"Here you are Miss Robinson," said the voice of Joseph from some seats behind me. I turned to see that he had procured a pair of skates for me, ladies ones that were built beneath a well-made high-ankled shoe.

"Those look very sturdy," I teased.

"I wouldn't have your exquisite ankles damaged miss," he grinned. "Let me help you."

I sat on the bench and extended a leg towards him. Joseph settled down onto one knee and unlaced my shoe, slipping it off and placing it by his side. I drew a long breath as he pressed the skate onto my foot in its place, and then pulled on the laces as he tied me securely in. I licked a lip and then held out my other foot in order for him to repeat the procedure. I watched him closely, relishing the intensity of his gaze whenever he lifted his eyes to mine.

You might think me brazen, and I fear your judgement in this telling, but please understand that I want you to understand the influence Joseph had over me at that time.

Suitably prepared I rose and moved carefully over to the

edge of the rink and held myself against the railing while Joseph put on his own roller skates. Then, together, hand in hand, we set out into the turning mass.

One of the great joys of taking an evening at the rink is the noticeable lack of Old Mother Grundy watching the young couples. I found my heart was racing from the excitement, the speed, and also from the proximity of my beloved Joseph.

"Isn't this amazing," I sang as we whirled around the curved end of the rink.

"Breath-taking," declared Mister Price, and he reached over to take my other hand, setting the two of us spinning around one another like dancers, rolling along the smooth floor.

I found my balance was slipping away from me, and I leaned into Joseph, catching myself on his shoulders. I could feel his figure pressed beneath my arms as I pushed myself upright again.

"I beg your pardon." I murmured, knowing my cheeks must be aflame.

"There is nothing to pardon you for Cora," he whispered, leaning close.

We paused on the rink and then a group of revellers flew by, spurring us to continue as well.

Eventually we tired and retreated to the seats that lined the rink. I sank gratefully onto one of the wooden benches and leaned back. I lifted a hand to my stomach and held it there as I attempted to catch my breath.

"Why Mister Price, would you not agree that this is the most agreeable way to spend an evening?"

"There are others." Mister Price's voice seemed unusual, different somehow. I started as he sat next to me and leaned closer, pulling one arm around me and pressing his fingers into my shoulder.

I tried to pull away and glanced at him, trying to figure out what had changed about his voice and behaviour. Then I saw his face, and recognised the same drawn and eager leer that had erupted during our previous evening together. Just as I had then, I was suddenly desperate to push him away, to make distance between us.

"Stop it!" I shrieked, and I clawed at the arm that was hooked around me.

Mister Price growled at the pain of my nails raking down his skin, and for a moment I was terrified to imagine that my efforts would not be enough, but mercifully he pulled away. I immediately took the opportunity to lunge to my feet and begin to flee, though the roller skates that remained on my feet made it difficult. Mister Price's own skates were also still attached to his feet, and so what followed was a pursuit that raised laughter amongst the various onlookers. None of them seemed able to recognise the fear that clutched at me, and I began to despair of receiving any aid whatsoever.

I tried to leave the rink entirely, gambling that some worker may chase me to reclaim the skates, and then I might be able to enlist their aid against this creature who had once been my Joseph. Before that could happen, I careened into a police officer who happened to be walking past the rink at exactly the correct time, nearing taking him off his feet. Which was you sir.

INTERVIEW WITH JOSEPH PRICE

Although I intended to make a full reckoning of my interview with the young man in the cell, regarding the accusations levelled by Cora Robinson, I found it extremely difficult to hold my attention upon his words. As he spoke I was overtaken by a feeling of revulsion, so strong that I wished to stuff my fingers into my ears in order to avoid being sullied by the very sound of his voice. However, I have noted his perspective to the best of my ability.

First of all, it is important to note that he does not contest the young woman's account in any meaningful way. He agrees that they met last summer and have developed a strong connection. He further agrees that this relationship was headed towards a formal declaration, although current events may have forestalled that possibility.

He states that he accompanied her to the skating rink as a popular destination for young couples and that he had no further unsavoury plans in mind when he chose it. However, where he diverges from the story of Miss Robinson is in his claim that his abhorrent behaviour was not in fact undertaken by himself.

This was difficult for me to follow, but he claimed that he was not himself when these actions occurred. He gives as evidence the description of his facial expression by Miss Robinson. He laughed and cried out "You see! I even looked like someone else! How can you suspect me of these things?"

When I confronted him with the evidence of my own eyes, he spread his arms and shrugged. "It was not me, not the Joseph Price who sits here before you" was all he could offer.

From what I can understand, he seems to believe that the history of Joseph Price, a well regarded and charming young man, simply cannot lead to the behaviours that Cora and I both witnessed. Therefore, it must have been the behaviour of someone other than the man in my cells, and it is not this prisoner who should suffer any repercussions for the behaviour.

CORA ROBINSON'S ADDITIONAL STATEMENT

I understand you have asked me to return in order to explain part of my previous statement, referring to another occasion where Mister Price appeared changed in my sight.

Less than a week ago, I had descended the steps outside my London home to the street. As the cold of winter drew closer, these afternoon strolls were running further and further into the darkness of evening, but I could not pass by the chance to enjoy a fiery sunset in the company of Joseph.

He was waiting for me at the foot of the stairs. He smiled broadly at me, and I felt my own smile spread across my cheeks in response. He extended his elbow and I took it lightly, enjoying the feel of his jacket and strong arm beneath my fingers.

"What a pleasure to see you again Miss Robinson," he said with a broad smile as I alighted the pavement beside him.

"It is always a sign of a wonderful evening when I am lucky enough to spend it in your company," I replied, equalling his smile with my own. I glanced over my shoulder and noted that my house-keeper was following us at a discreet distance.

At the end of the lane we looked out at the broad expanse of the circus, occupied in the centre by a large square pedestal with a bronze statue at it's top. Many couples were walking around it's edges, in exactly the manner that we intended to, and many other house-keepers and mothers were keeping a watchful eye over their charges. I chuckled softly. Even if one couple should stroll faster than expected, out pacing their own chaperone, they would find that they fell under the purview of another quickly enough. It was to be expected that each would report to the others.

In fact, as I watched, I saw two of the older women sidle up next to one another and tilt their heads closer, engaging in a conversation that caused raised eyebrows in both and a shaking of their heads. I giggled louder now.

"What is it?" asked Joseph.

"Nothing to concern yourself with sir," I answered, pressing his arm with my fingers to show that I was not intending to dismiss him.

We continued to stroll, chatting lightly about inconsequential matters and admiring the colours of the sunset. The sky began to glow as though the very gates of heaven were blazing only just beyond it's billowing clouds. The upper floors of the buildings around us seemed painted with fire. I leaned closer to Joseph and turned my head to the bright colours.

"What does this sight remind you of?" I asked lightly.

He turned his head slightly and then looked away again, focusing his gaze high on the colours that ran across the stone buildings beside them. He shook his head.

"I shouldn't say."

"Now you must!"

He grimaced but then opened his mouth. For a moment, no sound escaped, but then he began to speak softly.

"I must confess that my thoughts turned to the recent macabre news that has been gossiped about throughout the city. It shames me to consider repeating it to such a fine young woman as yourself, forgive me."

"Of course I shall." I looked up at the sky and knew immediately what was occupying Joseph. The newspapers had been full of accounts of the fearsome Edward Hyde, and the violence that he meted out upon the elderly and frail frame of Danvers Carew, M.P. The blood-red sky was naturally bringing the story to Joseph's mind. None of the papers had been able to say what was being done to call the brute to order, and I shivered. I hoped that the proper authorities would put that man in his place, whether that be the cells of prison or even six feet under! I recall blushing at the uncouth thought.

As the colours of the sunset drained out of the sky, I relished the darkness that followed. One by one the lamps that surrounded the circus were being lit, but shadows began to expand from the small spaces wherein they had been hiding. Each pool of darkness was a new potential space for me to catch a brief moment of true privacy with my companion. I felt my breath quicken each time we walked forward into another of the darkened spaces, potentially out of sight of the fluttering matrons who lined the circus, even if only for moments. After two or three, I turned towards Joseph and lifted my chin towards him.

However, the face that looked down on me seemed utterly unlike the smooth and charming face that I had come to know in him. His eyes were wide, and his forehead was lined with tension. A flush of blood to his cheeks darkened them, and his lips twisted in what I assumed was intended as a smile, but looked more like a rabid dog. His collar hung loose around his neck, as though the flesh within was shrinking away from the expression above. The sight turned my stomach. I was filled with a desire to put as much distance between myself and this being as I could.

"Sir!" I lunged aside, trying to avoid his outstretched fingers. They brushed against my upper arm, but I was able to spin away and step smartly back towards the light behind us. Two matrons turned their heads and stepped closer, their long noses and sharp eyes bringing to mind a pair of fussing black hens.

"Is everything alright my dear?" the first asked of me.

"Yes. No. I am not sure," I stuttered as I stepped gratefully closer to the pair. I looked over my shoulder, and saw Mister Price strolling after me, his face smooth and returned to it's usual demeanour, though concern arched his eyebrow.

"Are you alright Miss Robinson?" he asked as he approached. I moved closer to the older women, and they stepped forward.

"Has he been bothering you Miss?" asked the second, not taking her eyes from Mister Price.

Mister Price pressed his lips together but stepped away from the women, spreading his hands as a sign that he intended no harm. I studied him closely, tucking an errant strand of hair back over my ears. Then I sighed.

"I must have stumbled," I said slowly. "My eyes played tricks upon me in the shadows." I moved past the two black-clad women. They looked at me carefully, but then nodded and returned to their previous positions overlooking the circus.

"Very well. But don't you fear bothering us if you find that you stumble again."

"Indeed. We'll be very glad to be of assistance to you young lady. Is that clear young man?"

Joseph smiled and nodded, then offered his arm to me once more.

"Best you stick to the lit paths, if you want my advice," was the last remark directed towards us by the pair. I agreed. Although I was sure that Joseph was once more the safe and charming man that I had been spending so much time with, I was discomforted by what had just occurred. How the evening lights could have made my man's face twist in such a way, I could not explain. Why should a stumble have made me feel so vulnerable? What could explain the grasping nature of his reaction to my movement?

"I think I should like to return home now sir," I said, looking slightly down and straight ahead.

"Very well."

The rest of the week passed in good order, with no further disturbances to set me ill at ease, and I put the strange encounter away in my mind, thinking no more of it. I was so sure that I must have been mistaken. Perhaps Joseph had eaten something that disagreed with him, or maybe I myself had been ill?

OFFICER JACOB ANDERSON'S PERSONAL NOTES

The young woman I later found to be named Cora Robinson rushed out of the skating rink and crashed into me.

"Oi! What's going on here?" I yelled as I grabbed her shoulder and pulled her short.

"I do apologise sir, but this man is taking liberties and I need help!"

"What man?" I asked, only to look up past Cora into the oncoming fist of Joseph Price.

Cora screamed as the younger man struck me, causing many eyes to turn our way. I heard my own roar of pain, like that of a bear, but I did not fall. Instead I drew my wooden truncheon from my belt and whipped it up against the skull of Joseph Price, who grunted. The young man's eyes rolled backwards and then he fell to the ground like a tree being felled. Cora winced as his head bounced against the cobbles.

"What a bloody fool," I growled, rubbing my bruised cheek. I remember thinking, *that idiot will have me looking much the worse for wear.* I pursed my lips and looked back at Cora. "You'd better accompany me and this blighter back to the station," I said. "I'm going to need your side of the story, and I'm praying that it's a good one!"

Cora sat in the station with another officer, while I moved Joseph Price into a cell in the back. When I returned, I pulled out a pad of paper and freshly sharpened pencil.

"Begin," I instructed, and then proceeded to make as many notes as I could while Cora let me know the full events of the evening.

After taking her statement, and interviewing the young

man, I had to recall Cora in order to get some more information from her. After collecting all this information, I sent her home and wished her good health in the absence of Joseph Price.

The only sound in the station was the ticking of a small clock on the shelves to the side of the room. I could tell that my cheeks were flushed, and my nose wrinkled every time I thought about the case. I kept returning to the man's attempt at a defence, his claims that he was not himself.

I had turned the words around in my head ever since he had spoken them to me in his wheedling voice. My conclusion was that whenever someone claims that they are acting in a way that is unusual to them, or that they feel as though their actions were undertaken by somebody else, you may most reliably assume that these impulses had been merely hidden beneath the surface until finally bursting forth. Such men are pleased to imagine themselves separate from their own desires, from the evil that they perform. Maybe they really did have no history of indulging such awful whims, but I can say that they probably always wished that they could.

Their subsequent actions betray the lie to this claim of innocence. For should they have truly been acting beyond what they can countenance, should they not immediately give themselves up, or ensure that just punishment is brought upon them? No, these men seek absolution in the imagining that they are acting outside themselves, but in reality it is their absolute truth that they reveal in these moments.

THE DIARY OF CORA ROBINSON, JANUARY 20TH 18-

Today I was summoned back to the police station in order to give further information about Mister Price. It left me feeling utterly exposed, but I must hope that the facts will lead to his just punishment and not bring undue judgement upon myself.

However, once I left the station, I found the journey back home most unnerving. It seemed to me that each person I passed by along the streets wore the same look of clutching greed that had passed over Mister Price. Their eyes sought me out like a butcher seeks out a fine cut of meat, and each movement appeared to me as though the person was ready to turn and take me as their own possession.

The feeling only increased as I hurried home, twisting my stomach and making my skin feel as though needles were pricking across its entire surface. When I finally made it home I rushed to my room, where the feeling lessened and I was able to lay upon my bed and sob until the last traces of fear and suspicion washed away.

I pray that this feeling will not remain. I imagine leaving the house as I write this entry, and it grips my throat and breath. Will I ever feel safe amongst the world again?

Officer Anderson finished his drink with John, who clapped him on the shoulder and encouraged him.

"It sounds as though you caught a real trouble-maker, and saved a young girl from a sticky situation. Chin up Jacob, you are doing good in the world!"

Jacob nodded slowly, and then the pair stood and shook hands, agreeing to meet each other again soon. They left and turned opposite directions on the street.

Seated outside, holding a large glass of gin as he leaned back in his chair and watched John and Jacob passing by, a short stout figure began to laugh. The other outdoor patrons, all keeping a noticeable distance, turned unanimous scowls in the figure's direc-

tion. His low chuckle grew stronger and stronger until unbridled cackling suffocated the street.

DAWN

Have you ever woken to an angel on your pillow?
Her eyes will be closed,
her breath will be slow,
and if you are lucky,
she will share her dreams with you.

Yesterday was a blue day.
Bright and full of sun
that glowed like her soft hair.
Her hand rested on my cheek
as she shared her dreams with me.

DECOMPOS MENTIS

I do not know why I have such a fancy for this little café. Perhaps it is not the café itself, but the refuge it has given me for many years. Outside these comforting walls the world continues to progress, to change. Every year new problems I cannot comprehend seem to arise. Diseases from far countries, people brawling in the streets over who matters more. But in Maurice's oasis I can sit and smell the herbs covering the walls and pretend that life is just as it was in years past.

The walls wear antique mirrors, and planter boxes that overgrow themselves; spilling long leaves down the walls. I enjoy the life that Maurice encourages along the rough brick walls. Small ceramic pots sit on multitudinous shelves and green plants sprout like creatures reaching spindly fingers to pull themselves into our world.

Maurice still serves and smiles for every customer. Despite his thinning white hair and the way his eyes are beginning to cloud over, he has learned the names of all his regular customers.

"Good morning Sian," he says to me as I approach the counter. "Another cappuccino is it?"

"Yes please Maurice," I smile.

"Please, sit down. I will bring it to you in a moment." He gestures towards the simple wooden tables and chairs. I sit down and place my purse on the floor next to my seat. For a moment I slip my hand inside and touch the hard edge of my phone, but then I take a breath and pull my hand away. That's one of the things I love about this café. It has no wifi and it puts out free magazines and newspapers. It's as though Maurice is keen to slow down the world beyond the doorway. As am I.

I suppose that's why some small bright toadstools spread their frilled caps in pots on the shelves. Rings of toadstools are supposed to mark a passage from one world to another. Maybe these red and yellow domes are his way of marking the café as a separate world to the one outside.

The brightly coloured fungi are also a reminder of the slimy grey ones that he slips into some of his pasta dishes. I press my tongue to the roof of my mouth at the thought. It is a shame, but other people seem to enjoy the things. When I stand at the glass counter I ignore those off-putting dishes. Sometimes I wonder if other fungi would appeal more, like the fried slices of puffball I once saw on a British country living programme. Perhaps those giant white globes would be tastier. In the meantime, it's good that most of the sprouting caps in this café remain on the shelves on the walls.

A digital tone burbles from the doorway as someone walks in while using their phone. I watch them and it's like a cloud of spores drift alongside them. Seeds of that constantly changing world outside, floating into this safe haven. I imagine specks landing on my table and I wipe at its surface with a napkin, as though I can clean them away before they extend their threads into its surface and become impossible to clean out.

I lift my broad mug and sip at my cappuccino. The feeling of having to clean off the outside world makes me hope that Maurice is able to keep the fungus on the shelves under control. While I love feeling like I am sitting in an abandoned ruin, reclaimed by the forest after "civilisation" has failed, it would be disastrous if the fungi contaminated the food and drink of the café. I shudder.

There is a squeal from the far end of the café. Two small children are playing with a wooden kitchen playset, one telling the other that they are the customer and they must pay a hundred dollars for a muffin. The second child smiles and hands over a fistful of nothing. I smile and my eyes weaken.

Their hair lifts in blonde strings, fluffy as the fuzz that grows on old bread. I imagine these small happy figures growing older, arms and legs stretching thinner and thinner until their hands and feet suddenly inflate to catch up with the rest of themselves. My breath catches. My children Lily and Rory grew like that. I look at my phone, checking the time. The actual numbers vanish from my memory as soon as I place the phone back down, but the important thing sticks: They are late.

I used to bring my children to Maurice's café. It would have been them in the corner, building towers out of wooden blocks together. Then they would sit on the other side of my table, smiles splitting their smooth cheeks as they jammed spoons into their fluffies.

Fluffies, I think to myself. When was the last time Rory or Lily had fluffies? I recall the look on their faces as small ceramic mugs would be placed in front of them, white frothy milk piled up in each, a thick soft marshmallow planted at the top. The kids would dig their spoons in deep, leaving faces smeared with milk and sugar, and the tabletop only slightly less sticky. Those days are gone now. I lick my upper lip and exhale slowly.

I hear a car pulling up outside. It is cream coloured, and curves in soft waves. A man pushes its door open and emerges. For a moment, his face is smooth as a puffball, broken by weeping redness. Then I blink and his face is normal. I bite my lip and clutch my head in shaking hands.

That wasn't real, I tell myself. I've been by myself too much recently, that's all it is. My mind is playing tricks on me. Maurice walks over and places a hand on my shoulder.

"Are you alright Sian?" he asks. His eyes crease in concern. I nod and gulp down a mouthful of water from the glass on the table.

"I saw some things that- I think I miss getting to talk to real people. Too much chatting in Facebook groups recently." I look over my shoulder as the man comes into the café. His eyes are large and green beneath thick eyebrows. His mouth is thin but not unfriendly. I have no reason to think I was seeing anything other than a regular person.

"Perhaps you need another coffee, eh?" Maurice tries to smile but his eyes reveal that he is still worried about me. I shake my head, but he nods firmly. "Yes, another coffee. On the house." He goes to prepare my drink.

I slowly raise my head and examine the walls again. Green ferns curl up the bricks and still my panicked heart. Small rounded shapes press out from pots and branches. It is strange to think how the soft and flakey organisms are neither plants nor animals. It would be easy to assume they are plants, but I vaguely recall some definition that excludes them. In partic-ular I remember an article about a yellow mould that solves problems. I am sure there was an accompanying video, showing thick sticky strands of mould spreading in a glass rectangular case, pulsing and shining as the mould extended through the maze until it found the shortest route. Surely that thing showed animal intelligence beyond what a plant ever could? It was as though fungus was between one thing and the other.

Much like my children, I realise. They are no longer the small things playing in the corner of the café. They haven't even arrived in time for coffee. Now they have grown and spread, slowly expanding to take the form of actual adults, though they haven't fully formed yet.

They no longer smile at me when we come to the café. Instead, they stare at the phones they hold, and barely respond when I ask about their lives. Occasionally they lift their eyes to mine, glare into me, and tell me that I am outdated and paranoid! Over silly things, like a story I shared about a friend struggling with their staff demanding more pay, or a news article from Denmark talking about how parents could no longer put their daughters in dresses. It makes me so sad.

Even now, after this coffee together we are supposed to see a movie together, one Lily chose. She said it was 'an eye opening expose of the stigma that still disadvantages certain minority groups'. I sip from my mug. The trailer looked so dour. I didn't know if I would be able to sit through such a bitter film.

My eyes settle on the doorway to the café, the rectangular hole that leads back outside. I can see mould shadowing the edge of the doorway. That's unsightly, I frown. I smack my lips and rub my fingers together, trying to create a feeling of cleanliness that I know is unnecessary, but still...

Why would Maurice allow that? I look around the tall brick walls and the decorative hangings that adorn them. Glass crystals dangle, refracting rainbows, and potted flowers seem to glow from within. Such a beautiful café, I think, surely that mould needs to be cleaned up? But even as I watch, Maurice walks past the doorway to return a newspaper to the tray, where customers can pick it up. He folds it carefully in half, places it in the tray, and then smiles out the door at a young family walking by.

You must see it, I think. Grimy spots speckle the wall near the doorframe. Maurice scratches his chin and walks back to the counter.

Should I say something? I lean back and sip my hot drink. It tastes full and strong. I enjoy the mouthful. But the sight of the mould makes me uncomfortable drinking it. How can I be sure the kitchen is properly cleaned? The thought makes me feel guilty.

As I wait, I am grateful that Maurice brought me an extra coffee. Although I know it might leave my heart pounding harder than usual, it helps me focus myself and to ignore the dark smears that are encroaching on me. I was imagining things. I'm not really as abandoned as I feel. Isn't there a word for people who think that they see something wrong every-where? I shudder.

Maurice brings another cup of coffee to a young woman in a well-made blazer. Her blonde hair is pulled back into a pony-tail with a thin hair tie. She smiles up from her phone as Maurice arrives, and then places it on the table. I blink.

Black mould is growing out from where the phone lies, like a petri dish in time lapse. It is not so black as the mould around the door, but it is clear to me. I lift a hand to cover my mouth.

The mould brings revulsion to the back of my throat. I think about the mould that grew in the crevices of my bath-room. Only last weekend I had gouged out the darkened spots with an angular craft knife, separated infected rubber from clean, then scrubbed and bleached and disinfected what remained. Once the degradation was fully removed I could start afresh, returning the bathroom to the perfection of its early existence.

That is the only solution. Decay spreads where not driven

out. It hurt to think Maurice may not be able to drive out the spread within his café.

A jangle from the door to the outside. Finally, they've arrived! Lily sits to my right, then Rory sits on my left. I smile at my children but neither looks up from their phone. Are slick shadows spreading down their hands?

"Would you like a coffee?"

Rory and Lily shake their heads. My nostrils tighten. My fingers clench, as though I still hold the craft knife. I look at my children. They remind me somehow, disgustingly, of mushrooms.

SCARRED

The scar around my scalp feels peculiar,
a raised line of skin where the stubble of my hair
does not grow.

I have to pull my hands away from it
to stop tracing the path around my skull.

I talk with a thick tongue that pushes at my teeth
and write with heavy fingers that curl into cramp.

But I can see,
see you not looking.
And I can hear
every word that you whisper.

THE MAN WHO FISHED A WIFE

Once, many years ago, in a village far away, there lived a young man named Quiet. Quiet lived with his parents in a small house close to the river in a village called Riverside. Quiet never shouted or ran around like the other young men in Riverside. He never knocked down his younger sister so that she fell on piles of dirty laundry and began to cry, nor denied it if his mother shook her finger at him and told him off. Quiet preferred to find a nice shady tree and lie down to watch clouds pass overhead.

On the week of his eighteenth birthday, Quiet awoke to the sound of roosters calling from his neighbour's rooftops. In the living room, his father was sitting by the front door, watching the sun rise from behind the hill.

"Good morning son," he said.

"Good morning father."

"You will be a man soon Quiet," said his father, as he turned to look back into the house. "Soon will come the day when I will stop giving you chores for my house and you will have to run a house of your own. Will you be ready for the responsibility?"

"Yes."

"I am not so sure you are." Quiet's father frowned. "Have you been thinking about marriage?"

"Father!" Quiet complained. "I don't have time to think about that. The girls here are all awful." They were too loud for him, always with their mouths open and their high voices sounding like a flock of birds.

Modesty Manners was forever asking about his parents and their flocks and the chores he was doing. It seemed that he could never answer her enough to cease the questions.

Sympathy Holdfast was even worse. She would insist that Quiet was performing his chores in the least effective manner and would seldom leave him alone until he had completed them by her own methods. Quiet slumped lower in his chair.

"You're being cruel. There's nothing wrong with the girls in our village." Quiet's father watched the morning sky lighten. "Would one of the boys be more suitable?"

Quiet shook his head, he had no interest in the boys.

"Soon you will need to run your own home. It is much easier if you have someone there to help you."

His father sighed. "I worry for you Quiet. Now, listen to your chores." He listed Quiet's duties for the day. Quiet repeated the list before his father nodded and turned to leave. "Have a good day Quiet."

"You too."

Quiet wished he could follow his father. Most of the men in the village worked in the fields past the hill, and Quiet knew that he was meant to be out there, lying in the long grass, watching the flocks of sheeps graze, or running his hand through stalks of wheat. Instead he was trudging along the dusty street, heading west towards the well, to fetch water. He had two buckets with him, heavy enough that his shoulders were slumped though the buckets were empty.

As he walked, Quiet was joined by Modesty. She was carrying a basket, clearly fetching bread from the stalls near the well.

"Good morning," she chirped like a songbird that didn't know when to stop singing.

"Yes."

"Where are you going with your buckets?" Modesty's eyes narrowed slightly. "Are you going to the well?"

Quiet nodded.

"I knew it, I could just tell!" Modesty smiled triumphantly. "Well, I shall walk with you most of the way, as you can see I have to collect some bread for my mother, and the baker's stall is near the well. You see, my mother has been offering to feed old Mistress Harrow. Mistress Harrow has been extremely ill these last few days, and simply cannot be expected to feed herself. So my mother asked me to fetch extra bread today, and she is at home making some soup, and I shall deliver it later on this afternoon."

Quiet tried to ignore Modesty as they trudged through the village, but her voice vibrated like the highest trill of a flute. By the time they separated and he continued towards the well, Quiet was getting a headache at the back of his skull.

Sympathy was already at the well, tipping water into her bucket. She glanced up and raised an eyebrow at Quiet.

"Hello Quiet, what are you doing here?"

"I have come to collect water, as my father asked me to this morning."

"It is a poor time to come." Sympathy snorted. "The morning sun is reaching its height, and you will struggle carrying such heavy weights home beneath its heat."

Quiet sighed and shrugged, dropping his buckets and pole in the dust.

"You shouldn't drop them like that," she said, attaching her buckets to a long pole. "You might damage them and they will leak. You will waste so much water that way."

Quiet crouched and straightened the buckets.

"Is that your pole for carrying the water home?" Sympathy straightened and stood, the pole across her own shoulders bent at each end by the weight.

Quiet nodded.

"It doesn't look strong enough to me. I think that it will simply snap, and then where will you be?" She sniffed once more, then turned and walked away. Quiet reached one hand to the back of his neck and squeezed.

As he filled his buckets, winding the water up turn by turn, two more women came to the well to collect their own water. These were not girls from Riverside, but older women who had often guided Quiet in his youth. They spoke happily to one another as they approached.

"... a silly man, always trying to explain to me that his plans are going to pay off."

"After all these years?"

"Exactly as I said, after all these years. I do love him, but it would be much easier if he simply listened to me and did as I suggest."

"Oh, I know, my husband is the same. I tell him to mend the door and he says he will, but is then taken by surprise when the hinge breaks. Why did this happen to me, he moans as he repairs the door. It's all from not doing as I say, I think, but there's no good telling him."

Quiet murmured a greeting and finished collecting his water as quickly as he could. He wished that he could find a wife unlike the girls and women of Riverside. They were so loud, and always giving their partners so much to do. This was why he must join his father tending the sheep in the fields. Out there, no one would give him petty instructions, and keep him busily active from the time he woke until the time he went to sleep. No, he would be able to rest and relax, just as he dreamed. He smiled as he walked home with his water, picturing how wonderful life would be.

After he finished the rest of his chores, Quiet snuck out of the house with his fishing line and crept to the river.

It dawdled between the wide banks like a cat lazily unrolling itself in the sun. The water shone and glittered as it caught the light and Quiet's mouth spread into a comfortable smile. He found a smooth rock near the bank and sat down to prepare his line. The fishing hole was a pool so deep and wide that Quiet would often go swimming in it. Within minutes he had his feet resting on another rock, his hand nestled behind his head and his fishing line bobbing in the current of the river.

As the sun meandered across the sky, he checked his bait and tried different parts of the pool. Sometimes he would jiggle the pole to try and make the bait seem alive. By the time the sun was setting and he had begun to walk home, Quiet had caught nothing. He trudged through the cold forest with his stomach grumbling.

When his father came home, Quiet spoke to him.

"I can't wait for my birthday, so that I can come with you to work in the fields."

"Oh, is that so Quiet? Why do you rush to the fields?"

"I want to lie in the long grass, with a breeze on my face, and watch the clouds swim through the sky above me."

Quiet's father smiled, but said nothing.

As Quiet lay in his bed he looked out at the stars sparkling in the night sky. Among the constellations that his father had taught him, one star stood out. His father had named it Venus, the evening star. While he watched the star Quiet realised that his father never seemed to go fishing or hunting. He realised that it was unlikely that he would have much free time once he was married either. He called out to the stars, asking for their help and guidance. "Give me a companion who will allow me to enjoy the days of my life, and not be always rushed and busy."

On the morning of his birthday, Quiet woke to find his father had not left him any chores. And so, for the first time in many days, Quiet found himself a young man with nothing to do, watching a bright sun climb into a crisp morning sky. After such poor results the day before, Quiet was determined to catch a fish.

He gathered some bread and cheese from the kitchen, snatching up a small skin of wine as he did. He hoped that the fish would find the wine as appealing as the residents of River-side did. He retrieved his fishing pole from behind the house and began to untwist the line from the pole as he walked through the village. Some of the other villagers began to appear on errands of their own. Goodwife Manners was cleaning out her sheets, hanging them from a line strung between her house and her fence. Master Strong was setting to the repairs he was known for. Walking between the houses, giggling to each other behind their hands, were the girls.

Quiet ducked behind Master Tanner's house, avoiding the girls, and slipped into the low bushes at the edge of the village. Soon he was walking beneath the wide leafy branches of the forest, taking his time as he wandered down towards the river.

When he got to the fishing hole he uncorked the flask of wine and poured it into the pool. He watched the current pull the dark wine along the pool's edges. As he watched, he spoke.

"By the stars and fishes, may my wife-to-be bring me the same relaxation as I find here by this river."

After waiting a little while longer, he baited his hook and cast it into the water where the wine was darkest. Straight away he felt a tug on the line.

Quiet heaved on the line but whatever held onto the end of the line was nearly as strong as he was. Quiet was nearly pulled into the water himself. After a long battle, Quiet managed to pull the fish out of the water and it lay gasping on the rocks. Quiet examined it with pride.

The fish was gigantic, with long delicate fins. They were so fine that Quiet could see through them to the rocks beneath. The fish's scales were so small and so soft that they did not feel like scales but like a young woman's skin. When Quiet looked into the fish's large eyes he could tell that the fish was scared.

"What is the matter Fish?" he asked. "Are you alright?"

"No," the fish answered with a gentle woman's voice. "I am not alright. I have been caught by a young man who is looking at me with a strong hunger in his eyes. He will surely devour me whole for dinner when I should much rather be swimming in my river." The fish began to cry, great gasping sobs. Quiet did not know what to say. That was exactly what he had planned.

"I am sorry that I will eat you for dinner. I was taking my ease by the river, as it is all that I really want. But what else is to be done with a fish once caught?"

"Many things," cried the fish. "If you will marry me then we can live by ourselves. I would let you eat a small part of me each day, instead of my whole all at once. In return, I will keep you in such comfort as you have always dreamed!"

Quiet thought about this for a few minutes. This fish must be a blessing sent by the stars. He agreed. He would take the fish home.

When Quiet walked up to his parent's house, holding his

wife by her hand, her silver dress slipping around her long thin legs as she walked, his mother frowned at him.

"Quiet, who is this that you have brought home?"

"This is my wife," explained Quiet. He put an arm around the fish's shoulders. "I will pack my things, and we shall leave as soon as I can find us a home."

"Relax husband, " said the fish, pushing aside her pale hair with her hand. "You have had a long day. I will find a home for us."

And so for the rest of the day, while Quiet's mother prepared dinner, and Quiet's wife explored the village, Quiet sat outside the house, with a stalk of grass between his lips. He leaned back with both hands behind his head and watched the clouds passing by overhead.

When Quiet's father came home, he looked surprised.

"You appear to be sitting very calmly Quiet? Could you not be helping your mother with dinner, or chopping firewood for the winter?"

"I could," agreed Quiet. "But my wife is finding us a place to stay, and I wished to watch the clouds."

Quiet's father raised his eyes, but said no more.

Before the week was out, the couple had left to set up new lives in their new home. The house his wife had chosen was very comfortable, with plenty of wide long spaces for Quiet to lie down. Quiet began joining the other men in the fields with the sheep each day, laying in the grass between the animals and watching white clouds pass by overhead.

The other men would glare or grumble, but Quiet simply lay and smiled into the sky, before standing up at the end of the day and heading home to his wife. She always made him feel comfortable and he would eat a little of her for dinner. Each morning she would be up before him preparing break-fast and doing chores as he enjoyed the space and softness of the bed all to himself. Quiet was enjoying his new life very much.

One day Quiet was laying in the grass, running his fingers along the stems and stalks, when a blade of grass caught his thumb, leaving a small cut. As he sucked on the wound, he thought of the smoothness of his wife's scales. When he went home that night he ran his hand along her back only to find them as coarse as sackcloth. As he sucked on his sore fingers he asked why her scales were no longer as smooth as they once were.

"They couldn't stay that smooth if I'm not swimming in the river anymore could they? But that's okay because now I'm here for you." Quiet agreed that this was a very fair trade and told her how lucky he was to have a wife like her.

After the first year they were married, Quiet noticed that some things had changed in the small cottage. Instead of rugs on the floor, his wife laid down a layer of sand. To replace the small chairs and footstools in the house she brought in rocks. He didn't mind these changes as she was feeding him well every night. He continued going to the fields to lay in the grass and coming home to relax in his bed.

One evening his wife announced that they were going to have a child.

"What?" exclaimed Quiet. "Is that necessary? My life is so uncomplicated right now."

"Nevertheless," was her reply, and she continued to eat her dinner.

A few months later her proclamation proved true, and Quiet found himself the father of a small baby who bore a silver fish tail in place of its legs.

"You'll need to bring home more money," his wife told him, turning her head so one of her large bulbous eyes stared at him. He stammered and nodded.

Quiet found that the fields got busier and busier. He had been shocked by the lambing season. He had not expected there to be so much blood. He had looked forward to the shearing season, but found that he was hot and sweaty, covered in dust. He began to dread going to the fields.

Before the year was out, another child had been born to Quiet and his wife. She adored both children, playing with them all day, and barely speaking to Quiet any more. He found that there was no breakfast prepared for him when he awoke. There was no dinner ready when he returned at the end of the day.

"Why do you no longer feed me, wife?" he asked one evening, as his wife sat in a chair, bouncing the baby on her lap. It bubbled and gurgled through the large gill flaps on its neck.

"When should I make you this food, my husband?" asked his wife. "All day I am playing with the children, feeding the children, cleaning up after the children. Perhaps it is time that you learned how to cook for yourself, rather than simply expecting me to let you eat parts of me."

Quiet went to bed hungry that night.

The week of his birthday arrived and Quiet lay in his bed longer than usual in the morning. He listened to the shrieks of the children in the main room of their small house. Green curtains hung ragged over the windows. Twigs and leafy sticks poked out of the walls where they had been wedged. Quiet looked at the ceiling.

Work was much harder than he had expected. He had thought that he would be able to lay in the fields and admire the clouds. He would be able to enjoy the calm and the peace. However, that was not how things were.

His wife and children were louder than he had expected. He had thought his wife would take care of him for the rest of his life. He would have stillness and serenity in his home. However, that was not how things were.

Quiet thought about the last birthday that he had felt the tranquillity that he sought for. He remembered the day he had caught his wife, laying on the riverbank and watching the eddies in the water. He decided that he would go fishing again.

Quiet snuck out of the house early, picking up his fishing pole as he went. As he walked away from the noise of his children chasing each other, and his wife telling them to settle down, he felt a weight lift off his shoulders.

He turned aside from the path that would lead to the fields full of sheep, and began to walk down a track between the trees. A whistle came to his lips.

He sat on the side of the river and tossed his line in. The day passed in simple splendour. The sun above, the sound of insects lazily buzzing nearby.

He decided to go for a swim and dove into the river. He swam and swam, diving deeper and deeper under the water, until he decided to stay below the surface. He would not return to the difficulty and noise of Riverside. This was far more pleasant.

He swam through the river, reeds around him like long grass. His fins and tail slid him through the river with ease. The currents brushed past him like a breeze on his scales and he could watch the rippled surface of the river above him like clouds swimming through the sky.

Something flashed, shining ahead of him. He darted forward, curious to find out what it was. There was a sharp pain in his cheek.

The village downstream from Riverside told stories for many years of the giant fish they caught. They remarked to one another how tender its flesh was, and how satisfied they were after eating it.

NURSERY LIES FOR CHILDREN

Who should we listen to
Peter, Paul or Mary?
Peter and Paul are tricky birds
And Mary is so contrary.

Jack and Jill went up the hill
with schoolbooks in their hands.
Peter and Paul, the mockingbirds,
will stone them where they stand.

Peter Petros body-eater
picked a pickled papacy.
He drinks blood from dawn til dusk
between each calm decree.

Sleeping Beauty stepped on a crack
and dozed two thousand years.
Some fools say he's coming back,
but he's sleeping through our tears.

Magpie Paul beheld the sun,
gold coins upon the path.
He snatched it up all for himself
Ignoring poor folks' wrath.

Doubtful Tom the sceptic's son
look'd the holiest in his eye
and said, as he stuck in his thumb,
"What happens when good boys die?"

Mother Mary tends her garden,
plants pretty maids in a row.
But Bethlehem is bony dry,
and pretty maids never grow.

A wolf in shepherd's clothing
Pulls wool across our eyes.
He'll huff, he'll puff, blow down our walls
but never admit his lies.

So who is it you listen to?
Peter, Paul or Mary?
Peter and Paul use awful words
and Mary is awful scary.

Notes from the Author

One of my favourite things about short story collections is the little explanation of what the writer was thinking about when they wrote the story, or the ideas that they hoped that it expressed. So I have decided to include just such a section in my own collection! Don't feel that you have to read this, but if you are curious, here are some of my thoughts about everything I put in this collection.

If you would like to be informed of any new writing by me, try signing up for my Mailing List at: bit.ly/3kLKaaG

You can also find me on Facebook at: fb.me/AaronDickNZ

THIS QUIET ORPHEUS

About twenty years ago I was studying towards a Bachelor of Arts through Massey University's distance program and I took a creative writing paper under Bryan Walpert. One of the tasks was to write some poetry. My poem linked the planet Pluto to the classical underworld.

"This Orpheus Cannot Sing" took a scifi spin on the Classical Myth of Orpheus trying to bring his wife back from the dead. I really liked what I had written, but it didn't feel complete. Over the years I kept coming back to that poem, trying to add to it or change it to capture what it was missing.

Eventually I decided it needed to begin with the world that these people were trapped in, what sort of place would create these two people as they were in my poem. I thought I would be able to create a narrative poem, but that always felt like more was missing.

People suggested I change the perspective of the narrator, but I felt like the story hinged around the discovery at the end, and the leaving of obols for the dead to travel. I was always bemused by comments that gendered that narrator.

And so I kept adding more and more to it, trying to build out the world enough that it all felt balanced. And then I began sending it out to see if someone wanted to publish it. Over multiple years and 18 different markets, I sent it out.

Some held it but couldn't find the right space for it and eventually returned it to me. Some even rejected it with personal comments saying they enjoyed it, which was both heartening and disappointing. And then finally, this year, Headland decided that this story was one that suited them.

Headland is an online literary magazine run in partnership with the Massey University creative writing programme. They even had an interview with Bryan in Issue 19, a few months ago! So it feels right that "This Quiet Orpheus" ended up there.

EELS BITE DEEP IN LAKE PUPUKE

This was written specifically as an entry for a competition. The Australian Speculative Fiction facebook group called for submissions of stories that were tied essentially to a place. I thought immediately of Lake Pupuke and the Pumphouse theatre, as such an iconic place of my upbringing. But what sort of story would have to be set there? It would involve a performance, a show that reflects some part of the world to an audience that may or may not want to see that reflection. I thought of the demographics of the houses that lined the lake and that told me something of what would be revealed onstage, a thing that lies under the surface of New Zealand society.

THE VERY YOUNG GIRL

My friend Steffanie Holmes (who is a great author and you should consider looking up her books if you are interested in romance novels) shared a short story competition with me. It was being run by the Goethe-Institut Neuseeland, an organisation that promotes German language and culture in New Zealand. They wanted writers to take Grimm's Fairy Tales, and contextualise them to Aotearoa.

For me, that meant thinking of the key building blocks of so many of the Tales, and then swapping the particulars for New Zealand ideas. I tried to include the idea of threes, a symbolic threat that hopefully touches on truly deep fears in society, and the ability for cleverness to lead to success. All this was combined with New Zealand places, camping, and the threat of the possum.

I was thrilled that my story was considered good enough to

be included in the Anthology that the Institut printed, though it didn't win the competition.

SURFACING

I saw an anthology looking for horror stories that involved the ocean, and immediately pictured a quiet grey day out fishing from my childhood. The boat was small, and we didn't really even get out from the bay, but the drizzle made it feel so much quieter and alone than it would have on a summer's day. With that image in mind I needed to consider what awful things might be hidden in the dark water beneath the boat. Ultimately I discovered that the dark things were not in the water at first, but were being taken to be hidden there during the story.

BUTTERFLIES DANCE LIKE MOUNTAINS

I follow a man on social media who is a mapmaker from the Philippines. His optimism and love for his friends and his thoughts on maps and promotion of his indigenous people are all engaging and fantastic. But reading his posts sparked this story in my mind. It began with the pinning of a land into a specimen box, like a butterfly. I thought it would be about the usual short story length. Then it kept growing.

THE ALTAR

The Altar was one of the first short stories I wrote for the creative writing paper in my university degree. It was tweaked and changed over the years since then, until I put out my first small ebook collection and decided that it had to be finished.

The assignment gave the first line (the advertisement for

the wedding dress) and asked us to write the story of the dress. I, of course, immediately assumed the worst.

ORPHANS

A long time ago, two of my good friends Simon and Fiona decided to create a magazine that would highlight the things that they loved. Dark art, literature, fashion, heavy music, intense movies. Nocturne Magazine was a wonderful magazine, with fantastic articles and interviews, and the parties that accompanied each release were some of the most fun nights out I've ever had. I knew that I wanted to add to the magazine, but everyone else who was getting involved seemed so talented. Then one evening I sat down and wrote this story in one go, and sent it in to them. They accepted it, and though there are a couple of things I would consider changing if I was writing it now, I am still pretty pleased with it.

THE BABY WAS CRYING

My two youngest daughters are close enough in age that it felt as though I was waking multiple times a night to walk upstairs and settle them down, or feed them a bottle, for something like a decade. It was probably only a couple of years. But my sleep-addled brain, wandering through the house in darkness, conjured this situation one night and then it stayed stuck in my head until I got it out by writing it down.

AN EXPENSIVE JACKET

One of my next writing goals is to write something truly funny. Now, to me, this story is funny. However, I am aware that many people just find it weird. Maybe someday I'll figure out how to write funny.

I FOUND IT IN MY LETTERBOX

I tried to make this story shorter, many many times. Every piece of feedback I got mentioned that it was really too long. But I couldn't make it shorter without removing things that I thought it needed. Eventually I decided that Novelette was a reasonable category, and announced that that was what this story was, leaving it in the state that it was then.

One friend said that she found it quite unsettling to read, and was relieved when I said that it should have been unsettling!

OMENS

Nothing prompted this one. I sat down to write a story and could see the girl on the path clearly in my mind, and just how hollow she was, and I tried to figure out why she was there.

THE UNSETTLING CASE OF YOUNG JOSEPH PRICE

I saw a request for submissions to an anthology that was for new stories using many of the old classic monsters from Victorian writing. I remembered really enjoying reading The Strange Case of Dr Jekyll and Mr Hyde, and that Mr Hyde was not the "incredible hulk"-esque monster that he is so often portrayed as in modern versions. So I reread the original novella and then wrote my own story. In the original, the implication is that evil revealed by the formula is actually already present and part of the "good" man who uses the formula. For my story, I wanted to show that the world is already full of people who act as though they have taken Jekyll's formula, even if they didn't.

DECOMPOS MENTIS

A friend of mine pointed me towards a writing competition where you had to use the exact opening and closing line of another piece of work and create a new story from them. The year I decided to enter, they had said to use the first and last line of New Zealand writer Katherine Mansfield's "Je ne parle pas français". I really enjoy writing when I have been given some restrictions or requirements. Finding a way to work within that rule, and still create something that I feel proud of is the challenge.

THE MAN WHO FISHED A WIFE

Once, a very very long time ago, I got into an argument with someone and I was so upset that I got into my car and drove away. I had no destination in mind, just a desire to get away from the confrontation. As I tried to calm myself down so that I could go back and discuss what had happened, I tried to write down some story ideas and phrases. Eventually this odd folk-tale came together.

THE POEMS:

Most of the comments on my poems would be the same; I just try to describe a very specific moment and the feeling of being in that moment as clearly as I can. Because of this there isn't a lot more to say about some of them. If you can imagine what it would be like to sit in the moment that I described, then the poem did its job! I'll say a bit more about a few of my favourites.

Adoption - When I was living in Woodville, on the other side of the Tararua Ranges from Palmerston North, I remember standing in my cold house in the middle of a farm and watching as the calves were separated from the cows.

Drought - Standing on a dirt driveway in the middle of nowhere captured how I felt after my partner at the time and I had experienced a miscarriage.

Echo & Dawn - Poems about my daughter Annalise when she was young, playing in the garden and coming to stay with me.

The World Is Gone In Each Night's Chill & I See You - These are two examples of what happens when I try to write a love poem.

Triptych - I love the idea of seeing glimpses of a situation over time, and leaving the steps between them to the reader to work out.

Departure - Sometimes something that is supposed to only be a change feels like an end. Watching family leave to move overseas at the airport is certainly one of those situations.

Nursery Lies For Children - I really enjoy poetry with solid structure and rhyme schemes, though they often come out less engaging when I try to write them. I asked myself what sort of poetry suited those things and realised Nursery Rhyme was a perfect match. At some point I wrote a snatch of nursery rhyme parody that took images from christianity, and then I kept following that thread until the poem was done.

Acknowledgments

There have been so many people who have helped me with my writing, and I have to apologise if I forget anyone!

A lot of this writing has its roots in the creative writing paper I took while doing distance studies for my degree via Massey University. The lecturer there gave fascinating assignments and wonderful feedback, and the short lived community website that was formed by ex-students of the course helped me immensely.

My family and friends have put up with me talking about stories that never eventuated, and always encouraged me to keep going, and I am grateful to every one of them. Being able to pick up a physical book of writing that I made has been one of the greatest feelings in the world!

In particular, my friend Steff was an inspiration and a mentor, and I owe every book to her assistance. You can find out how amazing she and her books are by checking out www.steffanieholmes.com!

My friends Kat, Mark, Emma, John, Leanne, and Fleur have all been readers for many of the stories in this book. They gave me their impressions of what worked, what was too weird, and picked up the errors that inevitably creep into a pile of words this large.

Another amazing reader and editor I have relied upon is my mother Sue. She raised me surrounded by bookshelves and we have spent many evenings discussing books we read. She helped me learn as much as I could about grammar and how to put words together. She took me to readings by Terry Pratchett and Robert Jordan, even asking insightful questions about The Wheel of Time despite never having read any of the books. I'm lucky to have her.

Last but not least, my incredible and talented wife Andy has been my greatest cheerleader! I love her immensely, my life wouldn't be the same if I had not met her. She also did the artwork for the cover of this collection, and if you are interested in seeing more of her work you can look up Andy Dick art online. She uses the name Refractions of Light at the time of writing this.

About the Author

Aaron Dick is a teacher living north of Auckland in New Zealand with his wife, their two daughters, and a small menagerie of household animals. They all love when his eldest daughter visits too.

He grew up as a voracious reader of science-fiction and fantasy, often to the annoyance of his unheeded family. Becoming an author was a childhood dream, alongside being a palaeontologist, or a rock star.

You can keep informed of any new writing by Aaron, by signing up for his Mailing List at: bit.ly/3kLKaaG

You can also find him on Facebook at: fb.me/AaronDickNZ